G000166745

J.R. Mulholland was born and :
Germany, Scotland, England an(
Chesterfield, UK, where he met
and fell in love with rum.
www.jrmulholland.co.uk

Praise for *Hoist The Black Flag*.

'Absorbing adventure. It grabs you by the shoulders and totally immerses you in the treacherous world of 18th century piracy. J R Mulholland keeps up the pace of the first book with every twist and turn of this absorbing adventure. Grab a rum, sit back and enjoy. AH HAARR!'
Siobhan Rowden. Author of *Stardust Academy*.

'I can highly recommend this great second book of Pirate tales across the high seas. The author structured the scenes vividly and the historical language and context adds strength to the adventures of Dan Leake and his ramshackle shipmates. A great read to lose yourself in.'
Adam Bancroft. Reviewer.

'Another rip-roaring tale in the life of Dan Leake!!!!! This one will grab you and shake you so hard I can guarantee you'll get whiplash. You really get pulled into the story and I can tell you it doesn't let you go till the very last chapter. The story moves quickly and you really feel like you are there standing next to Dan and you really get immersed in the story, and to me that's all down to the author! J.R. Mulholland knows how to bring the characters to life right before your eyes.'
Lil-monster. Reviewer.

The Adventures of Dan Leake

HOIST THE BLACK FLAG

J.R. MULHOLLAND

J.R. Mulholland   Chesterfield

For my sister Siobhan,

whose encouragement and advice

have been invaluable.

<u>LIST OF CHARACTERS</u> (* Denotes fictitious character)

Calico Jack's crew:
*Algernon 'Scar' Lynch
Anne Bonny – Calico Jack's lover
*Ben 'Slugger' Sloane
*Dan Leake
*Gareth Griffiths
George Featherston – Bosun
James Dobbin
John 'Calico Jack' Rackham – Captain
John Davis
John Howell
John 'Old Dad the Cooper' Fenwick
Mary Read – Anne Bonny's lover
*McKaig
Noah Harwood
Patrick Carty
Richard Corner – Quartermaster
*'Spider' Stokes
*Thackeray
*Tom Bailey
Thomas Bourn
Thomas 'Needles' Earl – Sailmaker
Pettiagua crew:
Benjamin Palmer – Cabinboy
Edward Warner
John Cole
John Eaton – Captain
John Henson
John Howard
Thomas Baker
Thomas Quick
Walter Rouse
***Others*:**
Bartholemew 'Black Bart' Roberts – Pirate Captain
Captain Jonathan Barnet – Royal Navy pirate hunter
Dorothy Thomas – Fisherwoman
*Liam O'Connor – Indentured Servant and Slave Supervisor
*Lickspittle Leake – Plantation owner
Sir Nicholas Lawes – Governor of Jamaica
Thomas Spenlow – Ship's Captain
Woodes Rogers – Governor of the Bahamas

CONTENTS

Chapter 1   The Pirate Code   1
Chapter 2   Anne Bonny and Mary Read   15
Chapter 3   Enemies   28
Chapter 4   A Clue   36
Chapter 5   Plunder   47
Chapter 6   Duel   59
Chapter 7   Mutiny   66
Chapter 8   Cannibals   77
Chapter 9   Deliverance   88
Chapter 10   The Spanish Galleon   96
Chapter 11   Jamaica   109
Chapter 12   Lickspittle Leake   124
Chapter 13   Betrayal   137
Chapter 14   Captured   145
Chapter 15   The Trial   158
Chapter 16   The Gallows' Jig   174
Chapter 17   Gaolbreak   187
Chapter 18   The Pirate Captain   203
Historical Note   215
Glossary   219

CHAPTER 1

THE PIRATE CODE

The loud boom of a cannon jolted Dan Leake awake. He looked around in confusion, then remembered where he was. As he wiped the sleep from his eyes, Tom and Scar tumbled from their hammocks, stretching and cursing. After their ordeal, adrift in the sea, the few hours of rest they'd had wasn't nearly enough, and they were all still dog-tired. But at least they were warm, dry and, more importantly, alive.

Grabbing his jacket, Dan reluctantly followed his friends up on deck. A small merchantman lay ahead of them, a Dutch flag flying from her stern. The bow-chaser of the *William* fired again, putting a shot across the bows of the other vessel. But, instead of heaving-to and striking her colours, the ship's stern-chaser belched smoke, and a cannonball whistled over their heads.

"She wants a fight," yelled Calico Jack. "Let's give her a broadside before we board. Hard a starboard."

"Aye Aye, Captain," called the helmsman as he swung the *William* around to bring her larboard guns to bear.

Behind the gunners, row upon row of howling men

waved cutlasses and pistols, screaming curses at the terrified sailors scurrying around on the merchantman.

By Dan's side, Tom Bailey stared wide-eyed at the black flag that had been hoisted at the *William*'s mizzenmast. A death-white skull grinned down at them from its bitter perch on a pair of crossed swords.

"Pirates!" whispered Tom. "I can't believe we've been picked up by pirates."

Dan regarded the big, blond lad beside him. Tom was his best friend. Along with their gun captain, Scar, Tom had jumped into the sea to try and save him when he had fallen overboard from His Majesty's Ship, *Dover*. But the smirking bosun had ignored their cries for help and the ship had sailed on, leaving them alone in the wide Atlantic Ocean. Their joy at being plucked from the sea had been short-lived. They'd soon discovered the true nature of their rescuers.

"I'm sorry, Tom," sighed Dan. "I should never have got you involved in this."

When Dan's mother had died, he'd persuaded Tom to run away to sea with him, hoping to find his father who'd been pressed into the Royal Navy years before. It seemed like only yesterday that they'd shared their fifteenth birthday aboard the *Dover*, but now it looked as though they would never see their sixteenth. Saved from a watery grave only to find themselves at the mercy of a bunch of murderous cutthroats.

"I'm sorry," he said again.

"What do you mean, 'sorry'?" Tom's saucer-wide eyes darted from the Jolly Roger to the howling pirates. "This is great!"

Dan sighed again. Tom loved a fight, but he rarely stopped to consider the consequences.

All of a sudden the merchantman's flag fluttered to the deck, cut down by one of its crewmen. The ship turned into the wind and drifted to a stop.

"Hold your fire," called Calico Jack. "We don't want to damage anything valuable."

The launch and the jollyboat, loaded with jubilant, well-armed pirates, set off towards the other vessel under the protective cover of the *William's* guns. Dan, Tom and Scar were amongst the boarders, the captain testing their loyalty as the newest, albeit reluctant, members of his crew.

They reached the merchantman and scurried up the side like hungry cockroaches. The sailors offered no resistance. Half of them were English, and they pointed to the Dutch captain who they'd trussed hand and foot on his own quarterdeck.

A small nervous man spoke up. "It was him who f-fired on you," he stammered. "We b-begged him to surrender and refused to help him with the g-gun, but he fired it anyway. He was g-going to fire again, but we st-stopped him."

Calico Jack looked down his nose at the sailor. "So, there's only one brave man amongst you is there?"

The small man seemed to shrink even further. "B-but w-we…"

"Still, I can't have anyone thinking they can fire on Calico Jack and live to tell the tale, can I?" He strode over to the cannon. "Is it loaded?"

"Y-yes, sir. Apart from the ball."

A chain-shot, two cannonballs joined with a length of iron cable, lay by the muzzle of the gun.

"So, Captain." Calico Jack doffed his black tricorn hat to the man bound-up on the deck. "You want to fire the cannon again, do you? Well I won't disappoint you. Scar!" The big man pushed forward. "Help the captain up, if you please. Stand him next to his gun."

Scar effortlessly lifted the man to his bound feet.

"Hold him there." Jack turned away. "Thackeray!"

A fat, old pirate, nearly fifty years of age, hobbled up to them.

"Tie the noble captain to the chain-shot."

The Dutchman blanched but said nothing as his legs were firmly attached to the chain by a stout length of rope.

"Load!" called Jack.

One pirate eased the cannonballs, which were welded to either end of the chain, into the barrel of the gun. Another picked up a ramrod and forced them down.

The captain began to shake.

Calico Jack picked up a still-smouldering linstock from the deck and blew on the end. He passed it to the terrified captain. "Fire when you're ready, sir."

The trembling man looked pleadingly into Jack's hard face but, when he saw no mercy there, he straightened up. "Damn Je naar de Hel!" he shouted, and held the linstock to the touch-hole. The cannon erupted with a deafening roar and the captain was snatched from the deck. Dan watched in horrified fascination as the screaming man flew a quarter of a mile before plunging after the chain-shot and

4

disappearing beneath the waves.

The merchant seamen trembled, one of them throwing up over the side. Even the battle-hardened pirates stood in stunned silence.

"Wow," said Tom, bouncing on his toes as he watched the ripples die away. "That was grea..." He saw the look on Dan's face. "...gruesome. Really gruesome."

Calico Jack smiled at the captured crew as he strutted up and down in his striped calico jacket, his silver-buckled shoes glinting in the bright sunshine. "I need some volunteers," he said.

Every man took a step back.

Jack didn't bat an eye. "Is there a carpenter aboard?" he asked. "Our ship needs a carpenter."

The small seaman pointed out a tall sailor with short, ginger hair that stood to attention over a hang-dog face. "John Howell's a carpenter."

Howell scowled at him.

"Well John, are you willing to follow a new captain, or would you rather follow your old one?" Calico Jack looked pointedly out to sea and patted the cannon.

John Howell swallowed hard. "I'll follow you."

"Good man. I also need a decent cook."

A slim young man of about nineteen stepped forward. His short, black hair sat above a prematurely lined, weather-beaten, but not unpleasant face. His dark eyes were unflinching as he spoke. "My name's Mark Read and I'm a cook."

Calico Jack looked him up and down. "A good cook?" he asked.

The young man puffed out his chest. "The best. Had my own tavern in Holland in better times."

"What were you doing in the Low Countries?" asked Jack with interest. "Have you served in the army?"

"I was a soldier once," he admitted.

"Then you're welcome aboard the *William* As long as you're willing to sign the *Articles of Agreement*."

Dan frowned. There was that term again. Calico Jack had mentioned it when they'd been pulled from the sea, but then he'd been distracted by the sight of a distant merchantman and Dan and his friends had been allowed to rest after their ordeal in the ocean.

"I'll sign," said the young man.

His shipmates glared at him, bristling with disapproval.

"That's all the men I want," said Calico Jack. "I don't need the rest of you." He tapped the cannon as he spoke.

The sailors began to wail in English and Dutch, shouting each other down in their newfound enthusiasm to join the pirate crew.

Jack held up a hand for silence. "Don't worry," he said gently. "You're going to live. I want you to remember the name, *Calico Jack*. Tell people what you saw today. If a crew surrenders to me then they'll live. But if any man fights me, he will die, and he won't die easy. You can even keep your ship. This heap of woodworm and barnacles would only slow me down. All I want is your cargo."

The sailors slumped in relief.

Jack's eyes flashed with greed. "Now what is your cargo?"

"Bricks. Bleedin' bricks," complained McKaig, a wiry, one-legged Scotsman. "What the hell are we meant t' dae wi' bricks? Jack's useless."

"Aye, you're right for once," agreed Thackeray. "Jack Rackham may be bold but he's unlucky. What plunder have we had since we voted him captain?"

"Just bleedin' bricks," snarled McKaig. "We might as well have Charles Vane back as captain. He wasnae brave but we still took some silver in his time, no' just bleedin' bricks. By my reckoning we..." The Scotsman stopped in mid flow, his ginger hair bristling. "What dae ye mean, 'right for once'? Ye'll get my foot up yer arse if ye dinnae watch it!"

"Aye, maybe I would," growled Thackeray. "If it was still attached to yer leg!"

"Take that back ye slack-bellied, bilge-rat!"

Calico Jack sauntered onto the deck. He had some of the bricks loaded onto the *William* as ballast, indifferent to the grumblings of the crew. He approached Dan as he stood alone considering the cruelty he'd witnessed earlier.

"Why the dark looks, Master Sprat? Are you another one who doesn't like bricks, or is something else eating you?"

Dan had promised Scar he wouldn't say anything, but he couldn't help himself. "That poor man! How could you do that to him? You're nothing but an animal. You're a monster!"

"A monster am I? Tell me Master Sprat, how many men did you kill when you were aboard a British man-o-war?"

"I... I only..."

7

"Twenty? Thirty? More? You were a powder monkey. How many cartridges did you bring to the guns? How many times did they fire? How many men died?"

"But... but they were the enemy."

"They were still human beings and you sent them straight to hell, didn't you?"

"I was just doing my duty." Dan loosened the collar of his shirt. *He had done nothing wrong. And yet this pirate was somehow making him feel guilty.*

"And what of *my* duty, Dan. It's my duty to find plunder for the crew and to try and keep them alive while I do it. How many men did you say you killed?"

Dan remained silent. *He had done nothing wrong.*

"I killed *one* man," said Jack. "One! His death may have looked horrific - it was meant to - but his sacrifice will save many lives. Word will get around that Calico Jack is a ruthless, brutal murderer, but will show mercy to anyone who surrenders their cargo without a fight. How many lives will that save in the future? Even more than you've killed, I'll wager. Who is the monster, Dan? You or me?" He strolled back to the grand cabin, leaving Dan deep in thought.

Still angry and confused by his conversation with Calico Jack, Dan confronted Scar. When he'd first met him, Dan had been terrified of the gigantic, scar-faced black man, but he had taken the young Irish lad under his wing. He'd never said why. In fact he'd never said anything. They had thought Scar was a mute, but he had shocked them by speaking when the buccaneers had pulled them from the sea – the first words Dan had ever heard him utter.

"You knew didn't you?" Dan glared at the giant. "You knew they were pirates!"

"Scar knew. But better pirate than drown."

"I'd rather have taken my chance in the sea," snapped Dan.

"What chance?" boomed Scar, then pointed to the rail. "If you want swim with Jim Price, then jump."

After they'd been rescued, Price had wanted to throw Dan back into the water but, on hearing that he was from Cork, a slim young Irishman had stepped between them. When Price raised his cutlass, the smaller man had drawn a knife and slit his throat in one, blistering movement. The crew had tossed the body overboard without a second thought. Dan remembered the sharks dismembering the bloody corpse, and he shuddered. Caught between the Devil and the deep blue sea, he sank into a sullen silence.

"Sulk later," growled Scar. "Not much time. Listen now if want to live. Tell about *Articles*."

The boys said nothing so Scar went on. "*Articles* are pact between captain and crew. If sign, then you pirate and hang if captured."

Dan, folded his arms. "And if we don't sign?"

"They slit throat. Throw to shark. Life to them little value. Dan already see."

They sat in silence for a minute, Scar letting his words sink in.

Tom looked up at the huge man. "What are *you* going to do, Scar?"

"Scar sign. If ship captured, Scar say pirate force him.

Hope they believe."

"I'll not sign," said Dan through clenched teeth. "I'm not going to be a pirate. You saw what they did to that poor man. They're animals!"

Tom frowned. "Don't be stupid! You heard Scar. We've got to sign."

"I'm here to find my dad. He's in the Royal Navy. What would he think if he heard I'd become a pirate? What if he's in the ship that captures us? He'd have to hang his own son. I can't do that to him. I can't let him down."

"You're not going to find your dad if you're dead," snapped Tom. "Sign the *Articles*."

"No!"

The bosun, a big man with a thick neck and broad shoulders, called them over. Remembering his time in the navy, Dan glanced down at the man's brawny arms, half-expecting to see a knotted rope in his gnarled hands, but they were empty. "Ye've to come to the captain's cabin," he said, and led them to the stern.

"You have to sign the *Articles*," Tom hissed.

Dan shook his head.

As they entered the cabin, Calico Jack rose from behind a big, mahogany desk. Gaudily dressed in yellow and red striped calico breeches and matching coat, he dominated the room with his height and mere presence. Sharp, grey eyes regarded them from under a black, tricorn hat. "Ah, gentlemen," he said, taking off his hat and running a strong hand through the long mane of straw-coloured hair that framed his handsome, almost feminine face. "I have the *Articles of Agreement* here."

He tossed his hat onto the desk, reached over and pulled a sheet of paper from under a large, white paperweight. Dan recoiled. It was a human skull.

"I know the sprat can read, but what about the rest of you?"

Dan reddened, remembering the pirates' laughter when he told them that he could read and write. "I'm not a sprat," he snapped.

"Well, well," said Calico Jack, smiling. "A sprat with spirit. I like that." He handed the sheet to Dan. "Read it to your friends please, Master Sprat."

Dan snatched the paper, glared at the pirate, then began to read aloud.

"One. The Captain is to have two shares of any plunder; the Quartermaster is to have one and a half shares; the Mate, Gunner and Bosun, one and a quarter shares; the men, one share; boys, half a share.

"Two. He that shall be found guilty of cowardice in the time of action shall be marooned with a bottle of water, powder, pistol and shot.

"Three. If any plunder is not delivered to the Quartermaster in the space of twenty-four hours, the culprit shall suffer what punishment the Captain and the majority of the Company shall think fit.

"Four. He that should lose a limb in time of engagement shall have the sum of six hundred pieces-of-eight. One hundred for an eye or a finger.

"Five. He that shall be guilty of drunkenness in time of engagement shall suffer what punishment the Captain and majority of the Company shall think fit.

"Six. Lights and candles to be put out at eight o'clock at night. If any of the crew after that hour still remain inclined for drinking, they do it on the deck.

"Seven. Each man shall keep their pistols and cutlass clean and fit for service.

"Eight. No striking one another on board, but every man's quarrels to be ended on shore with sword and pistol."

Dan looked at the captain. "No striking one another on board? What happened on deck this morning, between Jim Price and that Irishman?"

"That one doesn't abide by the rules," said Calico Jack ruefully. "Now let's get the *Articles* signed." He picked up a quill and dipped it in an ink pot on the desk. "Algernon Lynch," he called.

Tom snorted. He'd only just found out that Scar's real name was Algernon. It didn't fit well with the big man's fearsome appearance.

Scar withered Tom with a look, then stepped forward and made his mark.

Calico Jack nodded to the human skull on his desk. "Swear you'll abide by the *Articles*."

Scar wrapped a massive hand around the skull and swore the oath.

"Tom Bailey!"

Tom took the quill and made his mark, then swore his oath on the skull.

"Dan Leake!"

Dan didn't move.

"Sign the *Articles*," hissed Tom. "They're decent rules, aren't they?"

"I'll not be a pirate," said Dan, his voice loud in the wooden cabin.

Tom groaned.

The captain regarded Dan coldly. "So you don't like our company then, Master Sprat? We can soon remedy that. You can go back to swimming, if you like? Sign the *Articles of Agreement*."

"No! I'll not be a pirate."

"Then tell me what use you are to us. How do I justify taking food from other mouths to feed you? You told me you're a powder monkey. Will you serve the guns?"

"I'll not fire on innocent ships."

Behind him Tom erupted. "Just sign the bloody *Articles*!"

Dan folded his arms, his jaw set.

Calico Jack stared at the small, dark-haired lad in front of him. The boy's earnest, blue eyes never wavered.

"I like you, Master Sprat. You amuse me and I admire your spirit, but you've got to give me a reason to keep you or the crew will throw you overboard. You have to understand that. They'll not carry a dead weight."

Dan said nothing.

The captain sighed and walked to the big stern window, staring out thoughtfully for a minute before turning back. "You'll not fire on innocent ships, but not all ships are innocent." His slate-grey eyes bored into Dan. "Britain is at war with Spain. Would you fire on Spaniards?"

Dan considered this. "I suppose so. Yes."

"Well now we're getting somewhere." Calico Jack stroked his recently shaved chin and nodded slowly. "I'll take you on as cabin boy — and part-time powder monkey whenever we can find some Spaniards for you to fight. And I'll see to it that you get all the dirty jobs on board. You understand if you'll not sign the *Articles* then you won't get a share of any plunder we take, and if we're caught they'll probably hang you anyway?"

"I'll take my chances, sir."

"There are no 'sirs' aboard *this* ship. You can call me Jack, or *Captain* if you prefer. George, show them around and explain their duties." Calico Jack dismissed them and went back to his desk as the bosun led them out onto the rolling deck.

CHAPTER 2

ANNE BONNY AND MARY READ

As the days passed lazily by, Dan's mood slowly lightened. The weather grew steadily warmer as they gently sailed south-west on calm seas. They soon fell into the easy routine of the pirate ship; quiet and relaxed compared to the noise, bustle and casual brutality aboard a British man-o-war. The sailors stood their watch without argument. They sailed the ship competently without the encouragement of a knotted rope across their backs. When Dan asked the bosun about discipline, he told him that no man slacked for fear of what his shipmates would think of him.

The 'dirty work' that Calico Jack had promised him, mainly consisted of helping the cook and doing the other men's dishes at breakfast and supper. The rest of the time he was pretty much free to do as he liked. It felt like a holiday compared to the constant drudgery on the *Dover,* or the daily battle to get enough food to eat before he ran away to sea. Free from the pointless holystoning of the deck that they'd endured in the Royal Navy, most of the day, when not involved in sailing or maintaining the ship, was spent in leisure. Men lazed about, playing dice or cards, while others carved strange sea-creatures from old lumps of wood. An old pirate drew a bow across a battered fiddle, as a group of sailors kicked out their legs in a drunken hornpipe.

The ship's timbers creaked in the gentle swell as Dan leant on the bow rail chatting with Tom. The salt smell of the sea filled his nostrils, and he smiled. He'd never felt so alive. Someone tapped him on the shoulder, and he turned to find himself gawping at the young pirate who'd stuck up for him when they'd first come aboard.

"Dan, isn't it?" The soft, silky voice didn't match the hard, green eyes.

Dan gulped, his throat suddenly dry. "Um, yes," he managed.

"I thought I told you to come and talk with me when you were free?"

"I've... um... been busy." In fact he'd been scared. He'd seen the slightly-built pirate cut another man's throat as casually as sticking a pig in a slaughterhouse. And he'd never seen anyone move so fast.

"Yeah! I can see how busy you are." The voice had gone cold.

"Err... This is Tom." Dan pulled his friend forward like a shield.

The pirate took Tom's outstretched hand and shook it. "I'm Anne Bonny."

"That's a funny name for a bloke," he laughed, ignoring Dan who was frantically shaking his head behind the pirate's stiffening back. "No wonder you ran away to sea."

"It's never bothered me." The voice had gone from cold to freezing. "Because I'm a woman!"

"What?" Tom's face dropped. "But I saw you... I mean... that other pirate! You..."

"So you think women can't fight, do you? Draw that cutlass and I'll soon teach you different."

Unlike Dan, Tom and Scar had been issued with sword and pistol.

"N-No," gabbled Tom. "I know you can fight. I've seen you."

Her cold, green eyes held Tom for what seemed like an eternity. "Well then," she said, suddenly turning her attention back to Dan. "Shall you and I have our wee chat?"

"I think you'd better say, yes," muttered Tom from the corner of his mouth.

Dan reluctantly followed Anne to the lee rail where she perched herself on a cannon and pulled the red bandana from her head. Long flowing locks of auburn hair fell down over her shoulders. He now couldn't believe he'd thought she was a man although, only minutes before, he couldn't believe she was a woman.

"So you're from Cork are you?" Her voice was soft and silky again.

"I am, though we moved to Bristol last year. That's where I met Tom."

"You're good friends?"

Dan nodded. "Tom looked out for me when I first arrived. Some of the local lads picked on me because I'm Irish and I'm not very big for my age. But Tom stood up for me. To start with I think he just used it as an excuse for a fight, but we hit it off. We make each other laugh."

"I'm not much of a one for the laughing, myself," said Anne quietly. "Never had much to laugh about."

Dan suddenly felt sorry for her. He couldn't imagine life without laughter, no matter how grim it might be. "Why did you become a pirate?" he asked.

"It just happened," she said. "My father's a lawyer, and we were doing well–."

"Your father's a lawyer?"

"Yes Dan, he's a lawyer. Anyway, we were doing well in America, but I was bored. Young, naive and bored. Things happened. I met Jack, ran away to sea and ended up a pirate."

"Just like that?"

"Not quite. It was complicated. What about you? What brought you to sea?"

Dan sighed. "My mum died so I was on my own. They pressed my dad into the navy years ago, and I've not heard from him since. I came to sea to find him."

Anne Bonny looked at him thoughtfully, pushing a strand of red hair away from her eyes. "Your name's Leake, isn't it? I knew a Lickspittle Leake once. He has a small plantation in Jamaica now, but he used to be in the Royal Navy. And Dan," she paused for a second, "he's Irish. He's from Cork."

Dan's heart jumped in his chest. His head swam. It might not be him, but it was the first lead he'd had since they'd set out. "My dad's called Daniel. I was named for him."

"It might have been 'Daniel'," said Anne. "I don't know. But his surname was definitely Leake. I won't forget that in a hurry." She scowled, but Dan was too excited to notice.

"What did he look like?"

Anne thought for a moment. "Tall, well-built, dark hair, blue eyes. He had a broken nose I remember, but he was good-looking in a rugged sort of way."

"That sounds like him. That could be my dad." Dan fumbled for the silver locket that he kept on a chain around his neck since it had once been stolen on board the *Dover*. It had been a present from his father to his mother and was the only thing of value Dan owned, not that he'd ever sell it. He clicked it open and passed it to Anne Bonny.

She studied the portrait. "I'm not sure. I've not seen him for some time. But yes, that could be him."

Dan grabbed her arm, his insides vibrating like a ship's halyards in a gale. "Are you a friend of his?"

"Er... Not exactly. But we have met. We were shipmates for a while."

"You were in the navy then?"

"No. I've never been in the navy."

"Anne!" Calico Jack was beckoning from the door of the grand cabin.

"Then how–?"

"Sorry Dan, I've got to go. We'll speak again another time."

"But–"

"Later!" She jumped off the cannon and swayed across the rolling ship and into the cabin.

Dan was in turmoil. He pressed his hands to the sides of his head as if it might burst open. *Was this 'Lickspittle Leake' his father? It sounded like him and he was from Cork. But his dad was in the Royal Navy so how could he have sailed with Anne Bonny? And he wouldn't have bought a plantation in Jamaica. If he'd left the navy he'd have come home to his mum and him in Cork, or tracked them to Bristol.* Dan's heart sank. It couldn't be his dad after all.

"What's up mate?" It was Tom.

Dan blurted out all that he'd heard from Anne. "It couldn't be him though, could it? I mean, how could he have sailed with Anne Bonny?"

"I've no idea mate. You'll have to ask her."

On the odd occasion that he saw her, Dan tried to speak to Anne Bonny about 'Lickspittle Leake' but she danced around the subject as nimbly as she'd avoided the slashing cutlass on his first day on board. She seemed to spend most of her time in the captain's cabin or in deep, intimate conversation with the young, pressed cook, Mark Read.

Dan felt a pang of jealousy as he watched Calico Jack teaching Tom to use a cutlass. They allowed him no weapons, but he was sure he'd done the right thing not signing on as a pirate. *He had to follow his conscience. It's what his dad would have done.*

"Don't use the point," Jack barked. "We're not on land. A rolling deck is no place for fancy footwork and a flicking point. You slash and cut. That's why we use a cutlass. Don't try to defend. One lurch of the ship and you'll miss your parry and be a dead man. Just attack. Faster than the other man. Cut and slash. Cut and slash."

Tom ignored the advice. He desperately tried to defend as Calico Jack drove him across the deck, beating him with the flat of his blade. Jack stopped his attack and shook his head. "Let's try again," he said patiently, and raised his cutlass one more time.

As the painful lesson continued, a low rumbling voice startled Dan from his daydream. "Scar tell why pretend not speak on *Dover*? And how got this?" The big man stroked the livid wound running the length of his left cheek.

Dan leant forward. With everything that had been going on since they'd joined the pirate ship he had forgotten his curiosity about Scar. The big man seemed to have said less since they knew he could speak, than he had on board the man-o-war.

"Scar runaway slave," he said gravely. "Run from Jamaica. Volunteer to sail in ship; work for free. But navy stop ship. Press Scar. If they know runaway, they send back, so pretend mute. Not risk words catching him out."

"For how long did you not speak?"

Scar held up two massive hands and extended all of his fingers.

Dan was nearly speechless himself. "Ten years! That's a long time."

"Now struggle to speak. So used to silent."

Dan realised that the big man had said more in one minute than he had in all the time that he'd known him. "And the scar," he prompted. "How did you get the scar?"

"Brand on cheek. When press-gang board, Scar take knife and cut it out so they not know slave."

Dan shuddered at the thought. Scar's life must have been a misery if he was willing to mutilate himself and hold his tongue for ten years rather than risk going back to slavery. "The English have been a curse to Africa," he said thoughtfully.

"Not just Africa," murmured Scar.

Dan was about to ask him what he meant when George Featherston strolled over. "Hello young Dan," he said cheerfully. "How are you settling in to life amongst a bunch of murdering cutthroats?"

"Well, Bosun," started Dan. "I–"

"Don't 'Bosun' me. Call me 'George'."

Dan could still hardly bring himself to call a ship's officer by name. "Yes, sir."

The bosun gave him a mock frown.

"George," said Dan at last. "I was thinking that life's a lot better than it was in the Royal Navy."

"Well don't go all rosy-eyed on us, Dan. We're on board for one reason only — plunder. The fact is we *are* cutthroats and murderers. All we're interested in is finding a rich merchant ship to loot. If they hand over what we want then all well and good, but if they try to fight you'll see another side to us."

"But you don't seem to be like that."

"Believe me we are. We just figure that when we're not at work, as it were, we might as well be jolly. We'll probably all hang but in the meantime we call no man master, we live a life of liberty and ease, we take what we want, when we want, and we don't go hungry. 'A merry life but a short one' as Black Bart Roberts likes to say. I prefer, 'A short life but a merry one'. It has a happier ring to it. Not that you want to meet Black Bart. He hates the Irish even more than he hates everybody else."

Dan agreed. He didn't like the sound of Black Bart, and he didn't want to meet him. He changed the subject. "Where are we heading... um... George?"

"Jamaica," said the bosun.

Jamaica! Dan's pulse raced. *Lickspittle' Leake was in Jamaica.*

Behind them, Scar scowled and stomped away.

The bosun glanced at the sun. "Nearly noon," he said. "You've had some education, haven't you, Dan? I'll show you how to take a reading with a back-staff, if you want? Maybe we'll make a navigator out of you."

"I'd like that," said Dan and followed him to the quarterdeck, happy to have something useful to do.

The bosun handed Dan the back-staff and showed him how to take a reading on the noonday sun, and plot it on the chart. "Of course, that only gives you the latitude. Finding the longitude is educated guesswork. So out in the ocean we spend most of our time more or less lost, or 'all at sea' as sailors put it." He picked a louse out of the seams of his jerkin and crushed it idly between his finger and thumb. "If we had an accurate timepiece then we could calculate it, but pendulum clocks don't work at sea with the rolling decks. Whoever invents a clock that works at sea will be rich."

"How do you estimate longitude then?"

"Dead Reckoning. We use the hourglass to give the time as close as we can, then judge sea-speed, current, and the strength and direction of the wind." The bosun laughed. "It's accurate to within a couple of hundred miles. If we're looking for an island, say, we'll sail along the latitude until we find it. The trouble is, if it's submerged rocks or reefs we're trying to avoid, we can't be sure where they are."

As George Featherston carried on his lecture, Dan regarded him closely. "How does a bosun know so much about navigation, if you don't mind me asking?"

The big man's eyes hardened. "I used to be a ship's master, but my captain was a sadist. Drove us all to mutiny. Now here you find me, a lowly bosun and pirate, but a happier man." He moved closer to Dan and lowered his voice. "But remember this Dan. Pirates are vicious and mutinous by nature. They'll cut your throat if it suits them. But most of them are uneducated. They'll always need a navigator. Learn the art and your life will be that bit safer."

Dan stood at the front of the quarterdeck, his head full of angles and distances, stars and constellations. Anne Bonny glided out of the cabin beneath him. He was about to excuse himself and go to speak to her when she once more latched herself onto Mark Read.

"What's her story, George? How come there's a woman on board?"

He lost sight of her momentarily as Tom retreated across the deck pursued by Calico Jack who was whacking him with the flat of his cutlass. "Don't defend. Attack," shouted the captain.

"What's her story?" echoed the bosun. "Now that would take some telling. You'll have to ask her."

"I never get the chance," sighed Dan. "If she's not in the captain's cabin, then she's with Mark Read."

As he spoke, Anne Bonny took hold of Read's hand, and they stared intently into each other's eyes as they talked.

George furrowed his brow. "She's sailing close to the wind there. Jack's the jealous type when it comes to women. He doesn't like to share."

"So Jack and Anne are married are they?" Dan felt slightly disappointed but wasn't sure why.

"Aye, they're married alright," said George. "Only not to each other."

Dan's mouth fell open. "But they're together?"

"That they are. She left her husband in Nassau and ran away to sea with Jack. They came on board together, him as quartermaster and her disguised as a man. No one knew. She cursed and fought like the worst of them. By the time we found out she was a woman, Jack was captain and no one cared to argue with Anne. She's a fearsome fighter. As for Jack, he's got a wife somewhere, they say."

Dan struggled to take this in. Back in Ireland, a wife wouldn't consider leaving her husband, never mind running away to sea with a pirate. He frowned and shook his head. After a while his eyes strayed back to Jack as he duelled with Tom. "How did he become captain?" he asked.

Tom advanced over the deck, slashing at the back-stepping captain. "That's better," yelled Jack. "But use the flat not the edge, you young scallywag. This isn't for real." Behind them Dan could see Anne Bonny and the cook still deep in conversation.

"We were sailing with Charles Vane," said the bosun. "We did alright under him, but then we came upon a French frigate. We outgunned her and Jack wanted to fight, as did most of the men. But in a chase or battle, the captain has the final word. So we ran. After that the men voted Vane out and Jack in. First thing Jack did was maroon Vane and fifteen men who stood by him." The bosun scratched behind his ear. "It's a risky job being captain."

A sudden shout and a flurry of movement, and Calico Jack was in front of Mark Read, his cutlass at the young man's throat. The cook remained stock-still while Anne Bonny pleaded for his life.

Calico Jack glared at Read, death in his eyes. "When I said you had free access to any meat on board, Mister Cook, I think you misunderstood me. Give me one reason why I shouldn't cut your throat."

Anne desperately tried to calm him down. "It's not what you think, Jack. It's not what you think at all."

"Enlighten me?" His voice was ice.

"Read's a woman!"

Calico Jack slowly lowered his cutlass. "What did you say?"

"This is Mary Read. She went to sea disguised as a man, just as I did."

"Is everyone aboard a bloody woman?" Jack roared.

Several pairs of surprised eyes swivelled around to stare at him.

"Bosun," yelled Jack. "All hands on deck."

George Featherston bellowed out the order.

Calico Jack cast a baleful eye over the hastily assembled crew. "Prepare to drop your breeches," he shouted.

The pirates looked around in confusion.

"Drop breeches!" ordered Jack.

"Should we no' put it to the vote, Cap'n?" blurted McKaig.

"No vote," screamed Calico Jack. "Drop your damned breeches."

At the back, Dan watched as row upon row of hairy arses appeared. Jack marched up and down the lines of puzzled men, then back up to the front. "Thank the Lord for that," he sighed and stamped off to his cabin.

The crew looked at each other, shrugging and muttering as they slowly pulled their breeches back up.

"The man's gone stark, staring mad," said McKaig.

No one argued.

CHAPTER 3

ENEMIES

Sweat poured from Dan as he toiled in the sweltering galley. He regarded the hard, leathery face of the cook as they worked. It was difficult to believe that this short-haired, tough-looking creature was a woman and that she was only nineteen, the same age as Anne Bonny. She glanced up and caught his eye. "Have a seat Dan. You seem all in."

"I'm all right. I'm tougher than I look."

"That wouldn't be hard," she laughed. He reddened, and she saw the flash of anger in his eyes. "I'm only teasing, Dan. No harm meant."

Dan hesitated. "Maybe I *will* sit down for a minute. The last few days have knocked me sideways. I hardly know who I am anymore."

"You're you, that's who you are," she told him matter-of-factly. "On a pirate ship you're allowed to be yourself. That's why I volunteered." She laughed suddenly. "Well that and the fact they'd have killed me if I hadn't."

Dan still smarted from her earlier teasing. "You're being yourself, are you? Pretending to be a man?"

Mary Read turned on him, lashing him with her tongue. "So I'd be being myself if I sat at home in a dress, spinning wool and waiting for a man to come knocking on my door, would I? Cleaning his house and bearing his brats for the rest of my life? That would be, 'being myself', would it?"

Dan flinched under the whip of her anger.

"There's little freedom for women in this world. They're slaves to their fathers, then slaves to their husbands, then slaves to their children. Only men are free, so I've lived my life as a man."

Dan gulped, his eyes on the ladle she had been using to stir a pot of lobscouse but had more recently been waving in his face. "How long have you been living as a man?"

Mary glared at him.

"If you don't mind me asking," he added hurriedly.

To his relief, Mary put down the big spoon. She stood motionless, staring back into the past. "Ever since I was a little kid," she said at last. She wiped her hands on her breeches. "My mother brought me up as a boy. It's a long story. Maybe I'll tell you one day."

She absent-mindedly twirled an imaginary ring on her finger, her hard face softening for a moment. "I did live as a woman for a while. Got married." Her expression darkened again. "But that's all in the past." She ran her still-greasy fingers through her short, black hair. "I decided to make a new life of it in America, and took a ship out there. That's when you and your mates attacked us."

"They're not my mates," Dan shot back.

"Aren't they?" Mary didn't sound convinced. "What about that handsome, young blond lad you're always hanging around with?"

"Handsome?" *They couldn't be talking about the same person.* "You can't mean Tom?"

"Tom! That's what he's called, is it?" The lines on Mary's hard face seemed to relax as she spoke the name.

"Well, yes. Tom's my friend, and so is Scar. We were shipwrecked though. Picked up at sea. We didn't set out to be pirates."

"You seem to be friendly with the bosun as well. And with Anne Bonny. And I've seen you chatting away with the captain on more than one occasion."

"Some of them seem okay," admitted Dan. "But they're not my mates. I'm not a pirate. I didn't sign the *Articles*."

"You didn't sign, and you're still alive?" Mary Read raised her eyebrows and looked at him keenly for a few moments. "Perhaps you're right Dan. Maybe you *are* tougher than you look."

They were another week closer to Jamaica when the lookout spied a sail. The ship sprang to life, and they sped after their prey with all canvass spread, the frenzied pirates baying for blood.

When the initial excitement had died down, and they settled in for the chase, Calico Jack gave Tom another lesson with the cutlass. "Pay attention," he warned. "Next time you use it will be for real."

When they'd finished, the captain retired to his cabin, leaving Tom leaning on his cutlass, panting and trying to get his breath back. Two pirates swaggered over and placed themselves either side of him. He recognised the bigger man as Ben Sloane. The bosun had warned the boys to keep clear of him. 'He's bad news,' is all he would say.

Sloane's mouth curled into a sneer. "I see the captain's got a new pet," he spat.

"Aye Slugger," wheedled 'Spider' Stokes, the scrawny, rat-like man on Tom's right. "He used to have a monkey, but this pet's uglier."

Tom bridled. "What's your problem," he snapped.

"We don't have a problem son – *you* have."

"You tell him Slugger. It's him that's got the problem." Spider Stokes' voice was a high-pitched whine in contrast to the deep growl of his friend.

Tom ignored the weasel and deliberately looked Ben Sloane up and down. He noted the knotted muscles in the arms of the burly man. Close-set, piggy eyes glowered over a broken nose, and a gap-filled mouth showed where past bouts of scurvy had claimed most of his teeth. Long, greasy black hair framed his pock-marked face.

"You don't look much of a problem to me," said Tom, raising the cutlass and resting it lightly on his shoulder.

Sloane took a step back, his dark eyes glinting dangerously. "You'll be seeing us around," he promised as he turned away.

"Aye," said Spider Stokes. "You'll be seeing us around."

"Don't forget your parrot," Tom called after Ben Sloane. Spider threw him a poisonous glance then scurried off after his mate.

Dan joined Tom, his eyes following the two pirates as they stalked away across the deck. "What was that all about?" he asked, his brow furrowed.

"No idea," said Tom. "But I think I've made a couple of enemies."

"It didn't take you long, did it?"

"It wasn't my fault, Dan. I was minding my own business when they came up and started on me."

Mary Read marched over. "Is everything alright?"

"Everything's fine," said Tom quickly.

"Ben Sloane's a nasty piece of work. And that little weasel Spider Stokes as well. Take my advice and stay out of their way."

"I can look after myself," muttered Tom.

Mary held his eyes. "Seriously," her lined face creased even more as she frowned, "Anne Bonny has been telling me a few stories. You don't want to get on the wrong side of them — not that there's a right side. If they give you any trouble let me know."

"I don't need mothering," snapped Tom.

Mary ran her fingers through his hair. "Believe me, Sweetie," she purred. "I don't want to mother you."

As Tom reddened she gave him a wink, smiling as she moved away.

Tom turned to his friend. "I'm scared, Dan," he admitted. "Really scared."

"Don't worry. I'll have a word with Scar. He'll sort them out."

"Sort who out?"

"Ben Sloane and Spider Stokes."

"Those idiots! I'm not bothered about them. It's Mary that scares me."

As they drew closer to the fleeing vessel it became clear it was just a small fishing boat. Mumbles of disappointment ran through the ship. A single shot across the bows, and the smaller vessel hove-to. The pirates lowered the jollyboat and once again Calico Jack took Dan, Tom and Scar with the boarding party, along with George Featherston, Anne Bonny and Mary Read.

They boarded the fishing boat without opposition. The owner of the vessel, a large woman answering to the name of Dorothy Thomas, wailed that she had nothing worth taking, only fish. Undeterred, Calico Jack had the jollyboat filled with fish. He also took all the fruit and vegetables they found in the galley.

"Jack's got this daft idea that fruit and vegetables can keep away the scurvy," explained the bosun, rolling his eyes and twirling his forefinger at his temple. "But every sailor knows that the only cure for scurvy is burying a man up to his neck in soil."

Their haul was taken to the *William*. When the boat returned for them, Calico Jack ordered the remaining pirates aboard.

"Just a minute," said Mary Read, pointing at Dorothy Thomas. "We're only a day's sailing from Jamaica. You're not going to let her live, are you? She could testify against us. Throw her overboard."

The big woman fell to her knees, palms pressed together as she pleaded for her life.

"Mary's right," agreed Anne Bonny, coldly ignoring the babbling woman. "We should leave no witnesses. We should kill them all."

A sudden iciness stabbed Dan's stomach. Two women he thought he knew were coldly demanding the death of another. His eyes flew over to Jack, searching for a spark of mercy.

"I don't kill women," snapped Jack. "We'll not be killing anyone. Now get in the boat. We don't want to be hanging about in these waters."

"We'll be hanging about on the end of a rope if you let them live," complained Mary Read, but they let Dorothy Thomas and her crew sail away unharmed.

Back on board the *William* the men were unhappy with their haul. McKaig stood in the middle of a huddle of pirates, bemoaning their fortune. "Bleedin' fish! Three months at sea and all we've got tae show for it is bricks and bleedin' fish."

Ben Sloane piped up. "If our luck doesn't change soon we should elect a new captain. Calico Jack is unlucky. We need a lucky leader."

The others murmured their agreement and grumbled the day away.

Dan sought out Anne Bonny. He'd come to like her and felt somehow betrayed by her casual, cold-hearted attitude to murder. The anger bubbled up in him like gas forcing its way through a swamp. "I can't believe you wanted to kill that woman."

"You think I don't value life, Dan?"

"I know you don't," he snapped.

"I do. It's just that I value *our* lives more than that of some old fisherwoman I don't even know. You've served in the navy. 'Messmate before a shipmate, shipmate before

34

a stranger, stranger before a dog.' Isn't that what they say?"

"That doesn't justify killing her. She was unarmed. What harm could she do?"

"She could have us all swinging by our necks, that's what. That boat is out of Jamaica. We'll be there in a day or two. One word from her, and we could be arrested as pirates."

"You *are* pirates!"

She ignored him. "We shouldn't have robbed her. It wasn't worth the risk for a few fish. We're too close to Jamaica. You don't mess on your own doorstep but, if you do, you clean it up. They had to die."

Dan shivered. "How can you be so cold?"

"It was Jack's fault, not mine. If I'd been in charge I wouldn't have robbed her in the first place so we wouldn't be having this conversation. But by being greedy and soft-hearted at the same time, Jack's put us all in danger."

"But you can't just kill people in cold blood."

"They'll kill us in cold blood if they catch us. You can bet your life on that. And don't think you'll be saved because you didn't sign the *Articles*. I've seen many a pressed man hanged when taken on a pirate ship."

The thought quickly cooled Dan's temper. His hand went to his throat. "You'd testify that I'm here against my will, wouldn't you?"

"Yes Dan, I'd testify for you. But who's going to take the word of a pirate?"

CHAPTER 4

A CLUE

The door to the grand cabin opened and Calico Jack appeared, rubbing his stomach and letting out a loud fart. He spotted Dan. "Ah, Sprat," he called. "My piss-pot needs emptying. It's nearly overflowing."

"You're joking," groaned Dan.

"I never joke about my piss-pot," Jack said with a straight face. "Now get it emptied. Or you could sign the *Articles* if you prefer? If you were one of the ship's company then you could tell me to empty it myself, but until that day you'll be on piss-pot duty. Well?"

"I'll empty the piss-pot," said Dan, his face screwed up as he anticipated the joys ahead.

"Suit yourself."

Calico Jack had been true to his word. The pot was nearly full and the foul liquid sloshed up to its lip with each gentle roll of the ship. Dan gingerly tried to pick it up by the handle, holding it out well clear of his twitching nose, but his arm gave way and he nearly spilled it over himself. He had to clutch the vile concoction to his chest with both hands to keep it level. The stench filled his nostrils, and he gagged as he made his way to the cabin door.

Out on deck he gasped in the fresh air but the gentle breeze did little to carry away the smell. Tom was lazing by the lee rail chatting with Gareth Griffiths, a laid back Welshman who'd found pirating easier than farming. He waved happily as Dan made his way to the heads to get rid of the pot's contents.

"You're doing a fine job there, Dan," called Tom. "I'd love to help you but I'm far too busy." He yawned and stretched out on the deck. "It's a pirate's life for me," he drawled, treating Dan to a smile and a wink.

"Up yours," Dan huffed as he carried on to the bow.

Tom laughed.

When Dan had emptied the pot he swilled it with seawater and took it back to the captain's cabin. Calico Jack was behind his desk again. He looked up as Dan came in. "Fine job," he said. "You're the best piss-pot emptier I've ever had. It would be a shame to lose you. Are you sure you won't sign the *Articles*? Our luck's bound to change soon?"

"No thanks," said Dan.

"In that case you'll be leaving us when we reach Port Royal. What do you plan to do?"

"There's a man I need to find. I heard he's in Jamaica."

"Well good luck with that. There are a lot of men in Jamaica who don't want to be found."

"This is different," said Dan. "I think he's my dad."

"There are a lot of fathers, and husbands for that matter, who don't want to be found."

"Not everyone's like you, Jack. My dad's a gentleman."

Calico Jack raised his eyebrows. "A gentleman, is he? Then God help you, Dan. God help you. And good luck with your search. It won't be easy out there on your own."

"I won't be on my own. Tom and Scar will be coming with me."

"Tom and Scar have signed the *Articles*. They won't be leaving this ship until we wind up the company and, unless our luck changes and we find a rich merchantman soon, that could be quite a while."

The colour drained from Dan's face. He'd assumed that Tom and Scar would be by his side as he set off to find his dad. Now it looked like he'd have to do it on his own. He swallowed hard. He suddenly felt very alone.

Dan realised that he'd have to find out everything he could from Anne Bonny before they reached Jamaica. If he left it any longer it might be too late. He found her in the galley, chatting with Mary Read.

"Hi Dan," they greeted him.

"Er... Anne, could I speak to you... erm... in private?" Dan felt himself reddening. *Why did he feel so awkward?*

"You can say what you like in front of Mary," said Anne. "We've decided not to keep secrets from each other."

Dan shuffled his feet. "I'd... erm... rather it was just the two of us."

Mary gave a deep, throaty laugh. "I think he's going to propose, Anne."

Dan's ears grew hot, and he looked down at the floor. *Why did women have to be so difficult?*

"I'm sorry, Dan," said Anne.

Well at least she wasn't as bad as Mary.

"I can't marry you," she went on. "I already have a husband — and a lover or two." Her eyes caught and held Mary's for a moment. She turned back to Dan. "My love life's complicated enough without adding you to it, sweet as you are."

Dan closed his eyes. "Can I talk to you or not?"

"Anything for you, Dan," she said, taking him by the arm and leading him away. "I like a masterful man. See you later, Mary."

The cook waved them off as if they were setting out on their honeymoon.

Ruddy women.

Out in the sunlight they found themselves a quiet corner of the deck. Anne regarded him thoughtfully, her head tilted to one side. "What's so important that you have to drag me out here on my own?"

"It's about Lickspittle Leake," said Dan.

"Oh, him!"

"We'll be in Jamaica soon. I'll be leaving the ship and I may not see you again."

"That'd be a shame, Dan." She squeezed his arm gently.

"Yes, well, um, I need to know everything you can tell me about him. I've got to find him. He might be my dad."

"Okay Dan, I understand." Anne let out a sigh. "From what I've heard he has a small plantation near Port Royal. If you get there and ask around, someone should know where he is – if he's still using his own name, that is."

Dan furrowed his brow. "Why wouldn't he be using his

own name?"

"A lot of people in Jamaica use an alias."

"Why?"

"Well, they've all got their own reasons. He's probably not changed his name anyway. Forget I said it. Most people don't even bother these days."

Dan stared at her, his eyebrows knitted together. *She wasn't making any sense.* "Is there anyone else who might know him?" he asked hopefully.

"Lots of people knew him, but most of them are dead."

Dan sighed. *Was she being deliberately obstructive or did she really know so little?* "You said you sailed with him. Tell me about that."

"Not much to tell. He was a…" Anne paused, searching for the right word, "…an associate of my husband. They sailed together for a while and I joined them briefly on a voyage before I fell out with my darling hubby."

"Tell me about the voyage — about Lickspittle Leake."

"When you find him," said Anne, "if he is your father then you'll have to ask *him* about it."

Dan pressed, but she held up a hand. "Ask Lickspittle," she said. "Sorry I couldn't be more helpful."

'Or wouldn't,' thought Dan.

Anne Bonny sat down on the deck and lit a clay pipe. She offered it to Dan, but he waved it away and said, "Can I ask you a personal question?"

She smiled. "If you don't mind a personal answer."

"You're married," Dan started.

"And?" Her tone cut through him like cheese-wire through a chicken's neck.

"It's just... I mean… How come you're with Jack?"

Anne's voice was cold. "And why's that any of *your* business?"

"It's not. I just…" Dan looked away. "I'm sorry."

"You're shocked, aren't you?"

"No! I mean, yes. I mean…"

Anne's tone softened. "I'm sorry, Dan. Living this life I sometimes forget how prudish the rest of the world is. Always looking for shackles to chain you with." She lowered her head but then raised her eyes to gaze into his. "And I sometimes forget you're just a kid."

Dan's eyes were twin daggers. "Don't ever say I'm just a kid. I may not be a cold-hearted killer like you, but I have lived. You're just a poor little rich girl playing at pirates. You got to choose your life. I've had to live mine as best I can. I've had to look out for myself. I've gone hungry. I've robbed and stolen so I could eat. I've seen death and I've killed but, unlike you, I still value life."

Dan had shocked himself with his outburst, but he realised that he was right. He wasn't a child anymore. He hadn't been for a long time.

"Well, well!" Anne leant back and puffed on her pipe. "I wasn't expecting that, so I wasn't." She sat forward again and blew out a stream of smoke. Her eyes caught Dan's. "But if I'm not to judge you, then neither should you judge me. Not until you've heard my story."

Dan slowly relaxed. He felt the anger draining from him as he sat down beside Anne Bonny and listened to her strange tale.

"I wasn't born a poor little rich girl, as you put it. It's

true that my father had some money. He was a respectable lawyer in Cork, with a respectable wife and a respectable business. The trouble was that my mother wasn't so respectable. She was a maid in my father's house. They say that she seduced him, but they would say that, wouldn't they?"

Dan didn't know what they would say, so he kept quiet.

"Anyway," said Anne. "She got pregnant and my father hid her away and paid her an allowance. Nine months later I made an appearance. After a few years, he took her back as a maid again and pretended that I was a relative's son he'd hired as an apprentice. So I was raised as a boy."

She looked at Dan but again he didn't know what to say and so said nothing.

Anne carried on. "Well his wife found out and made a big fuss, so my dad moved out and lived openly with my mother and me. This wasn't done in Ireland. It was alright for a rich man to get a maid pregnant, but he was supposed to dismiss her and leave her to starve, not move in with her and his bastard child and look after them. Our good Christian neighbours weren't going to put up with that sinful act of charity. They ostracised my mother and avoided my father's law practise. His business went broke. We moved to America where he made good. So yes Dan, maybe I did become a poor little rich girl."

"And what happened in America?" asked Dan, intrigued in spite of himself.

"My mum died." Anne swallowed then carried on. "My father was busy all the time, building up his business. I guess I was left to run wild. But I was bored. I wasn't much older than you when I met a young sailor. His name was James Bonny. He was handsome and fun, and he told me tales of adventure on the high seas. It turned out he was a small-time pirate but I didn't know that back then. My father saw straight through him though and wouldn't let us marry, so we eloped and went to sea with me disguised as a boy. When my father found out and cut me off without a penny, James Bonny suddenly lost interest in me. When we got back to shore he tried to sell me at a wife auction."

"Sell you?" Dan gasped, his eyes widening.

"Women are scarce out here. Anything scarce is valuable. The auctions aren't legal, but they still go on. Anyway, the governor found out and put a stop to it."

"Your husband tried to sell you just because you had no money?"

Anne smiled to herself as she thought back. "Well he did catch me in someone else's hammock, but it was the money he cared about."

Dan's mouth fell open.

"Now I *have* shocked you," she laughed. "I don't live my life by others' rules."

Dan closed his mouth. He still couldn't think of anything to say.

"By the time the governor intervened, Jack Rackham had already bought me. The Governor ordered my release but I thought to myself, who do I want to be with — the man who wants to sell me or the man who wants to buy me? So I stayed with Jack. Do you understand that?"

"I guess so," said Dan.

"The governor didn't. He threatened to have me whipped for adultery, so I ran off to sea with Jack who went back to piracy. I soon took to the life. It's the only true freedom there is. You might come to realise that one day."

Dan thought about this. "If the price of freedom is preying on others then I don't want it."

"Rich merchants, that's who we prey on. Don't think they don't prey on us, because they do."

"That fisherwoman wasn't a rich merchant."

"No she wasn't. Like I told you, I wouldn't have robbed her. That was Jack's call and it was a bad one. He's a good man in some ways, but a fool in others."

She left Dan to consider her words and made her way to Jack's cabin.

That evening the crew ate a supper of fried fish and fresh vegetables. Dan sat between Tom and Scar and watched McKaig wolf down the meal.

"Bleedin' fish!" moaned the Scotsman, wiping a dirty sleeve across his mouth. "We need a captain who can catch mare than bleedin' fish."

Tom looked pointedly at McKaig's empty plate then rolled his eyes at Dan. They grinned at each other. Scar was as silent as he had been on the *Dover*.

As they ate, Ben Sloane walked around their table, deliberately catching the back of Tom's head with his elbow as he passed. "Sorry pet," he said as Tom jumped up. "Accidents will happen."

"Aye," said Spider, at his side as usual. "Accidents *will*

happen. You can bet on that."

Scar slowly stood up, as far as the low-beamed ceiling would allow. Sloane and Spider hurried away.

"Thanks, Scar," said Tom. "But I can fight my own battles." The big man said nothing but sat down again and stared at his plate.

"We'll be in Jamaica by this time tomorrow," said Dan, pushing his food around his plate with his knife. "I'm going to Port Royal to find this, Lickspittle Leake. See if he's my dad, or if he knows him. Cork's not that big a place. If he's not my dad, he'll have heard of him."

"I'll come with you," said Tom.

"It's not that easy, Tom. You and Scar have to stay with the ship's company until you're released."

"You've been at sea too long, Dan," chirped Tom. "I think you've got salt water in your ears. I said I'm coming with you. What about you, Scar?"

Scar didn't look up. "Jamaica? Already said. Runaway slave. Won't set foot in that place."

Tom hesitated then spoke up. "Jack's thinking of basing us here for a while — hunting these islands." He glanced up at Scar. "You may have no choice."

"Always choice," said Scar through clenched teeth. "Whatever have to do, Scar do it."

Dan's scalp prickled as the big man spoke. He hadn't realised just how strongly Scar felt about this place. "You know," he said. "It may sound strange but ever since you two jumped into the ocean after me, I thought that somehow we'd always be together. I still think that. I can feel it deep inside me. Somehow this will all work out."

"Maybe in next world, not this." Scar rose and shuffled away, hunched under the beams.

Tom patted Dan on the back. "Don't worry mate. We'll stick together, you and me. Just try getting rid of me."

"Thanks Tom," said Dan as he regarded Scar's retreating back. "That's good to know."

Sleep didn't come easily to Dan that night. His mind jumped from concern about Scar to elation at the thought of finding his dad, then down into gloom again. *This Lickspittle Leake couldn't be his father, could he*? He eventually drifted into a fitful sleep where he tossed about in a churning ocean of dreams, until the morning light heralded another day.

CHAPTER 5

PLUNDER

The lookout stirred in the crow's nest, suddenly alert, staring into the distance. "Sail ho!" he cried.

"Where away?" called the bosun. Calico Jack had yet to emerge from the grand cabin.

"Two points off the starboard bow," cried the lookout.

George Featherston studied the horizon through his spyglass. He straightened up. "McKaig!" he shouted. "Wake the captain."

"But the captain's sleeping," grumbled the Scotsman.

"I know he's sleeping," yelled the bosun. "That's why I need him waking?"

"He doesnae like to be woken up. He–"

"Just wake him, blast your eyes!"

McKaig stomped off to the cabin, his wooden leg clunking angrily on the timber deck. Two minutes later Jack hurried onto the quarterdeck, doing up his calico breeches. Mary Read arrived just after, her hair dishevelled.

"What is it George?" asked Jack, his eyes sparkling. "A merchantman?"

"Looks like it." The bosun passed him the spyglass.

"She's a merchantman alright." Jack snapped the telescope shut and paced the deck. "How far from Jamaica do you think she is?"

"Not far enough. Must have just left port. By my reckoning Jamaica's just over the horizon."

Calico Jack stopped pacing and stared fixedly at the distant ship, his forehead wrinkled in concentration. "Set all sails, George. We'll chase her down."

The bosun frowned. "She's too close to shore, Jack. We'll be seen."

"Let's worry about that when the time comes. We've got to catch her first."

"But, Jack…"

The captain stopped the protest with a wave of his hand. "We'll put it to the vote, if that will put your mind at ease?"

"Okay Jack," said the bosun, shaking his head. "We'll put it to the vote."

The *William* bit through the waves, eating up the distance to its quarry. Dan gripped the bow rail and peered ahead, the outline of Jamaica now clearly visible between the green sea and the light blue sky. Dan's eyes swept over the distant land, his mouth dry and his whole body trembling. He was now convinced that Jamaica was the key to finding his father.

"Well, there she is," said Tom, putting a hand on Dan's shoulder. "We're nearly there."

Dan swallowed hard. He had almost given up believing in his dream, but now it was so close he felt he could reach out and touch it.

Beside them, Scar stared at the dark shadow of land on the horizon. "Prayed never see that accursed place again," he said in a near whisper. A shudder went through the big man and he stepped back as if to put more distance between himself and Jamaica, but the *William* moved relentlessly closer.

The bosun's voice rang out. "That ship's not making her way out to sea. She must have seen us. She's waiting under the protection of the shore batteries."

"I think you might be right," said Jack, pulling off his hat and scratching his head. "We'd better lower some sail – make a more leisurely approach. We don't want to spook her. Oh, and run up the Red Ensign. We'll bamboozle her. Make her think we're a British merchantman."

The bosun raised his voice. "Lower topgallants. In with studding sails. Raise the Red Ensign."

The topmen jumped into the rigging. Tom winked at Dan and scampered up after them, balancing on a swinging foot rope in the topsails as he helped to furl the foremast topgallant with both hands. At his side, old Thackeray glared at him, appalled by his youthful disregard of danger.

"Remember, young 'un," he called as the rigging snapped and cracked around them in the freshening breeze. "One hand for the ship and one hand for yourself." Thackeray hung on with one hand and deftly rolled the canvas with his other.

"*I'm* alright, old man," laughed Tom still working two-handed. "But what's an old dog like you doing up here? Shouldn't you be helping the cook at your age?"

"Mind yer mouth ye cheeky young pup," shouted

Thackeray. "Remember this. A topman doesn't learn by his mistakes. One mistake and his brains is dashed out on the deck. Ye learn from yer elders and betters."

"Yeah, yeah," said Tom. "You just hang on tight old 'un, and I'll do the work."

A sudden gust hit the ship and she rolled violently. Tom's foot slipped and he let out a cry, wind-milling his arms, desperately trying to keep his balance.

Thackeray reached out and grabbed him, steadying him until Tom got both hands onto the sail spar. He clung to it gulping in great swathes of air.

"Thanks," Tom eventually blurted out. "And I'm... I'm sorry for what I said."

"That's not a problem, son. Like ye noticed, there's not many old dogs up here. That's coz most topmen die young. Ye need to learn that the only way to grow old is by not dying young. There's no other way." Thackeray grinned at the cocky lad now hanging onto the rigging with a death-like grip. "Now I'll just be off to help the cook. Ye can make yer own way down."

He clambered away leaving Tom still clinging to the spar like a drowning man to a plank of wood.

When Tom eventually climbed back down he found Dan at the bow, still staring out at Jamaica. Tom glanced around. "Where's Scar?" he asked.

"Gone off to be on his own. I'm worried about him. Seeing Jamaica has changed him. I mean he has always been so..."

"Scary?" offered Tom.

"Unshakeable. He's like a rock. I thought nothing

could ever move him, ever frighten him."

Tom glanced up at the rigging. "I used to think that nothing could frighten *me*. Until I met you."

"What!"

"No, I don't mean *you* scare me. But the things that have happened to us recently? When we first went to sea I remember telling you I wouldn't use the heads and I'd hold it until we got to shore. Sometimes lately I've been so scared that I'm lucky if I reach the heads in time, never mind the shore."

Dan gave a half smile but said nothing, his eyes still on the distant land.

"I guess what I'm saying is that we've all got something that scares us. Even Scar. There must be something that scares *you*?"

"I used to be scared of most things," said Dan. "But now my only fear is that I won't find my dad. That seems to have blocked out everything else." He took a deep breath and closed his eyes. "It makes me feel guilty sometimes. I mean, I can't wait to get to Jamaica. I'm sure it's the key to finding my dad. I know how much Scar dreads the place, but I just push that to the back of my mind."

Tom put his hand on Dan's shoulder. "Look Dan, the whole reason you're here – the reason we're here – is to find your dad. You're right not to let anything else get in the way. For you it's the most important thing. More important than Scar. More important than me. Just focus on finding your dad. Scar and I will be alright."

"Thanks Tom. You're right." But even as he said it he

began to suspect he might be wrong. *He couldn't just abandon Scar and Tom, could he?* He bit his cheek. "I find my dad first and worry about anything else later, right?"

"You do that Dan. You do that."

They were closer to Jamaica now. Dan could make out individual trees and scattered huts on the shore. Calico Jack had come up to the bows to try to get a better look at his prey. Through his spyglass he could now see the name of the merchantman they were after. "She's the *Kingston*," he cried. "She's low in the water. Laden with goods."

A murmur of excitement rippled through the ship from bow to stern.

As they drew nearer they could see the *Kingston* had lowered her sails and anchored close to the harbour of Port Royal. Her captain obviously suspected that the *William* was a pirate — not an unreasonable assumption in Jamaican waters. He must have felt safe under the shore batteries of the town and, before setting out on the lawless high seas, was waiting for the ship to pass by or put into port.

Calico Jack called the crew together. "Right lads," he cried. "There's a rich merchantman ahead, ripe for the plucking. I say we pluck her?"

The pirates roared their approval.

George Featherston stepped forward and vainly held up his hands for silence. "Listen," he shouted above the clamour. "We're too close to Port Royal. We'll be seen. They'll come after us!"

The crew ignored him, and carried on cheering and shouting. George tried again. "There's no point plundering treasure if we don't live to spend it!"

"Treasure!" shouted Calico Jack and the pirates cheered louder than ever. He smiled smugly as the bosun gave up with an exasperated sigh and stood down. "Who votes we take the ship?"

"Aye!" The cry was deafening.

"Now shut up and get out of sight. This has got to be done by stealth. I want everything to look above board."

The pirates slowly calmed and, still talking in excited whispers, took cover behind the bulwark, under the ship's boats, and in the fo'c'sle and hold.

"See that they're all armed please, Bosun." Jack spotted Dan by the rail. "Except for Master Sprat of course. Cutlasses, clubs and pikes only. No firearms. I want this done quietly."

"It won't be quiet enough, Jack," grumbled George. "You've always had more courage than sense."

Calico Jack stiffened, his hand on the hilt of his sword. "There's a chase on. Are you going to carry out my orders or not?"

"Aye Aye, Captain," said the bosun, shaking his head at the folly. "I'll see that they're all armed and ready."

Dan crouched behind the starboard bulwark with Tom and Scar, as the *William* inched closer to the *Kingston*. A skeleton crew sailed the ship. The rest of the company, armed to the teeth, hid out of sight.

Tom thumbed the edge of his newly sharpened cutlass, wincing as he drew blood. His feet drummed on the deck as he leant back against the bulwark, his eyes gleaming. "You should join us Dan. A proper merchantman at last. We'll be rich after this."

Dan stared open-mouthed at his excited friend. "You're not a pirate, Tom! You only signed on to save your neck, remember?"

"Um… Oh, yeah!" Tom's face lit up as a thought struck him. "But if we make good money then we'll be released from the ship's company and Scar and I can help you look for your dad. That's… um… why I'm excited."

"Scar not join you," growled the giant black man.

"Okay Scar," said Dan sadly. "I understand."

They were within hailing distance of the merchantman now. Calico Jack raised a speaking trumpet to his mouth. "Ahoy there. We're *Albatross*," he lied. "Bound for Port Royal with a cargo of slaves."

"*Kingston*," replied the ship's captain. "Bound for England."

"What's your cargo?" called Jack.

The captain's voice stiffened. "And what business is that of yours?"

Calico Jack cursed himself for raising suspicion in the other man's mind. "No business. I just want to know a good cargo for the return voyage."

The captain of the *Kingston* did not reply.

"We've got three men on board," called Jack. "Washed overboard from a British man-o-war. We picked them up mid-Atlantic. They're anxious to get back to Britain before they're posted as dead or deserted. Would you take them on board? Give them passage to England?"

"Aye," replied the captain. "I could do with three honest hands. Port Royal's a nest of vipers. I had to turn down most of the cutthroats who tried to sign on. Pirates to a man by the look of them. Lower a boat and send them over."

The *William* edged ever closer to her prey, the hidden pirates jabbering in excited whispers, weapons clutched tightly in eager hands.

"My boats have been damaged," called Jack. "May we come alongside?"

The helmsman reacted to his cue and swung in towards the merchantman. The pirates waited in a ferment of silence now, hearts thumping.

The captain's voice rose in alarm as the *William* bore down on them. "Permission denied," he shouted. "Bear away. We'll send a boat for the men."

Jack played for time as they closed on the *Kingston*. "I'm sorry, I couldn't hear you. Could you repeat it?" He held the speaking trumpet theatrically to his ear, head tilted to the side as he pretended to listen for a reply.

"Bear away," bellowed the captain. "Bear away!"

They thudded into the *Kingston* and the pirates leapt up from behind the rail, flinging grappling hooks and fixing her tight in their grasp. Men in the rigging flung pikes onto the merchantman, pinning the dying captain to his own quarterdeck.

Tom and Scar jumped up and followed the screaming pirates as they swarmed onto the other ship. Dan watched from the *William* as they cut their way through the *Kingston*'s crew. He saw Tom exchanging blows with one of the merchant sailors. He fell at Tom's feet and Dan gaped as his friend ran on, waving his blood-soaked cutlass and bellowing along with the rest of the pirates.

He closed his eyes for a second, silently praying for his friend's soul. When he opened them again he saw Anne Bonny and Mary Read at the forefront of the battle, fighting their way viciously onto the enemy's quarterdeck where the ship's officers still fought on around their fallen captain. The first mate thrust a sword at Mary Read. She swayed aside, bringing her cutlass slashing down, severing the man's arm at the elbow. As he screamed and clutched the mangled stump, Anne Bonny plunged her knife into his neck and pulled it violently back, ripping out the man's throat in a fountain of blood.

The two women moved on, Anne fighting with skilled restraint, Mary hacking and stabbing like a mad-woman, her lips pulled back in a rictus smile that froze Dan's blood.

In a matter of minutes it was all over. The surviving crew members threw down their weapons and begged for mercy. A few were killed but most were allowed to live as the pirates blood-lust slowly abated. They locked them in the cabin then the whooping sea-robbers poured down into the hold to check for loot.

On board the *William*, George Featherston stood beside Dan, looking towards Port Royal and slowly shaking his head. "Jack's a fool," he said quietly. "We'll have been seen. Shots or no shots, them on shore will know our business sure enough. They'll not fire for fear of hitting the *Kingston,* but we'll be running for our lives before the day is out."

Dan's blood ran cold. He put his hand on the rail to steady himself. "Do you mean we won't be landing in Jamaica?" *This couldn't be happening.*

"Not a chance," said the bosun. "We'll be heading away as fast and as far as we can."

Dan gazed longingly at the shore and tears jumped into his eyes. *He was so close and yet...* He ran to the fo'c'sle and flung himself down in a corner, his head in his hands. For the first time since he'd been on board the pirate ship, he wept.

"Jack!" the bosun called over to the *Kingston*. "You have to get the men back on deck. They can count their plunder later. We need to get out of here, now!"

"Aye, you're right," said Calico Jack, and he ordered men to cast off the grappling hooks. "Make for *Isla De Los Pinos*. I'll whip these greedy dogs back on deck, and we'll follow you as soon as we can get the canvas up."

The bosun bellowed at the remaining crewmen on the *William*. "Cast off. Helm over. I want the wind on the larboard beam. Topmen, prepare to trim sails."

The ship came to life as the skeleton crew rushed to their duties, and they pulled away from the captured merchantman.

Calico Jack kicked and punched the plunder-struck pirates back on deck and up into the rigging. Forcing reluctant men to set the sails in an unfamiliar ship took its time, and the *William* was leagues away before the *Kingston* finally picked up speed and sailed after her.

Their activities had not gone unnoticed in Port Royal. Local merchants, whose fortunes were tied to the

Kingston's cargo, quickly announced a reward for her return. Before she had disappeared over the horizon, three well-armed vessels cleared the harbour and silently set course after the retreating pirates.

CHAPTER 6

DUEL

Dan sensed that the ship had come to a stop though it still gently pitched and rolled. The rattle of the anchor chain running out through the hawse-hole confirmed it. He emerged from the fo'c'sle into the fading light of early dusk. *Kingston* and the *William* were anchored in a wide, tree-fringed bay with a long shore of black sand stretching away into the distance.

"*Isla De Los Pinos*," said the bosun. He leant against the starboard rail and gazed at the shore. "The sand is black because of the volcano, but the fresh water's clear and sweet. We'll rest and re-fill our water-butts here."

Dan didn't care where they were, or what colour the sand was. His only concern was getting back to Jamaica. He felt a desperate need to talk to Tom.

"George, is there any chance of me going aboard the *Kingston* tonight?"

"Sure," said the bosun, scratching at an itch in his armpit. "If you don't mind swimming." He spat into the sea. "There's sharks in these waters though, and they like to feed at night."

Dan swallowed hard. "Well I'd better get on with it before dark then, hadn't I?"

The other ship was only fifty yards away but it looked a long, long way to Dan as he balanced on the rail and peered down into the dark, brooding waters beneath him. He took a deep breath, hesitated a second, then jumped.

Despite the warmth of the sea, he felt a cold shiver as he bobbed to the surface. He thrashed his way through the water to the *Kingston*, every nerve in his body screaming. He reached the side but could find no way up. He felt the panic welling up in him. "Ahoy the ship," he called, his eyes darting around.

A rhythmic tapping came towards him then McKaig's surly face appeared at the rail. "What dae ye want," he shouted. "It's past four bells."

"Throw a rope!" yelled Dan, anxiously treading water.

McKaig stared down at him. "Do ye ken there are sharks in these waters? I wouldnae be out for a swim, if I were you."

"Just throw a rope, you tow rag!"

" 'Tow rag', is it? I'll give ye, 'tow rag'," muttered the Scotsman.

A few minutes later, a tow rag dropped down the side of the ship. Dan grabbed hold of the attached rope and hauled himself out of the sea, stopping and panting for breath when his legs cleared the water. Slowly he climbed to the top and pulled himself over the rail. McKaig was grinning. Dan wasn't sure whether to thank him or choke him, so he just ignored him and went to look for Tom.

"Ungrateful pup," he heard McKaig chuntering behind

him.

Dan could hear raised voices coming from the fo'c'sle. He pushed in past dozens of rum-sodden pirates. They'd been helping themselves from the *Kingston's* well-stocked hold. Trouser pockets clinked with silver coins pilfered from the rich cargo. Several men sported new straw hats, and one shimmied by in an expensive dress arguing with Anne Bonny who was trying to claim it for herself.

He spotted Tom, face twisted in fury, nose to nose with Ben Sloane. "I'll take no more from you, Sloane," he shouted. "Either draw your cutlass or keep your big mouth shut."

Ben Sloane slowly drew his cutlass.

"Go on Slugger. Skewer him. Cut his gizzard out," snarled Spider Stokes as Tom drew his own sword.

Men jumped back, forming a human ring as Tom and the burly pirate circled each other.

Thackeray stepped between them. "*Ship's Articles!*" he bellowed. "No striking one another on board, but every man's quarrels to be ended on shore, at sword and pistol."

Ben Sloane smiled and lowered his weapon as Tom hesitated, uncertain.

"That's easily sorted," growled Sloane. "The land's only two hundred yards away. We'll settle this on shore like it says in the *Articles*. Barking irons and cutlasses."

"Any time," spat Tom.

"Noon tomorrow then. I like to do my killing after a good lie in and some breakfast."

"It's me that'll be doing the killing!" Tom's chin jutted towards the pirate, the cutlass flexing in his grip.

"Save it for tomorrow," cried Thackeray. "Dan, take yer friend out on top would ye? Let him cool off a bit."

Dan took Tom by the arm. "Come on mate. Leave it for now."

"Tomorrow then," Tom flung over his shoulder as Dan led him from the fo'c'sle.

Out on the darkening deck, Dan threw his hands in the air. "I can't leave you alone for a minute without you getting into trouble, can I?"

"It's him who's in trouble," barked Tom, blowing out a noisy breath and crossing his arms.

"You haven't listened to anyone, have you? Sloane's a killer. Didn't you see him when you took the *Kingston*?"

"Yeah, he's great against defenceless men, but I'll be armed. And anyway, I did alright myself."

"Killing innocent sailors? You call that doing alright?"

Tom's jaw set stubbornly.

"We can talk about that later," snapped Dan. "Right now we've got to get you out of this fight."

"I'm not backing down. I've had enough of Ben Sloane. I'm going to fight him and I'm going to kill him."

"Have you ever even fired a pistol?"

"You point it and you pull the trigger. How hard can it be?"

Dan sighed and shook his head. "I'm going to see Scar. He'll sort this out."

"Don't you dare! I fight my own battles. If I back down now I'll look a fool."

"You *are* a fool."

Mary Read came down from the quarterdeck where

she'd been eavesdropping. "I thought I told you to come to me if that 'un gave you any trouble?" she said gruffly.

"And I thought I told you I could look after myself," snapped Tom. "Push off and leave me alone."

"What time do you fight?"

"Noon tomorrow. Why? What's it got to do with you?"

"I don't want to miss him killing you," hissed Mary as she marched off.

At dawn the pirates began to stir and look out to the tree-lined shore. The thought of dry land and fresh water drew them like magnets. Empty water-butts, along with full barrels of rum, were piled into the ships' boats which made repeated trips to the beach until only Dan, Tom and a handful of hung-over men remained on board. On shore the rum barrels had been broken open and the boys could hear raucous shouts, and even a pistol shot, as the pirates cut loose. Dan and Tom were amongst the last to make the trip to the black sands.

Dan studied his friend who sat stiffly in the bow of the boat. "There's still an hour to go, Tom. It's not too late to back down."

"Back down? You know me better than that, Dan. There's no point trying to talk me out of it. You'd do more good if you gave me a bit of encouragement."

Dan took a deep breath then slowly released it. "Okay, Tom. Good luck!"

"Oh! Great! That's really buoyed me up. Can't wait to get at him!" Tom shook his head. "Can't you do better than that?"

"You know I'm on your side Tom, but I can't pretend to be happy about a stupid duel where you're going to get yourself killed."

"That's more like it. That's made me feel far better. Thanks a lot!" Tom swatted at a fly that buzzed around his head. "Anyway, it's not stupid!"

"Why not? What's it about?"

"Well he… um… he said… well..."

Dan looked hard at him and Tom shrugged. "Okay. It *is* stupid, but I'm still not backing down. He's been spoiling for a fight and he's going to get one."

The two boys sat in strained silence until they reached the shore. They splashed out into the surf and helped pull the boat up above the high-water mark. As they walked along the beach towards the main body of pirates, Dan noticed the way they looked at Tom. He'd expected to see sympathy or encouragement, or at least excitement, in their faces but no, it was more a look of resentment — or scorn.

"What's up with them?" grunted Tom, his nerves strung tight.

"I've no idea," said Dan, his brow furrowing. "I didn't think Ben Sloane was popular, but you don't seem to have many supporters."

They drew near to where the pirates gathered. Dan came to an abrupt stop when he saw the object of their attention. Stretched out on the blood-soaked sand lay the body of a man. Tom saw it at the same moment. "What the…!"

They moved closer and the pirates, cold stares following the boys, parted to let them through. One spat in Tom's direction. On the ground at their feet, eyes staring sightlessly upward, a neat hole in his forehead, lay Ben Sloane.

"I… I don't understand," stammered Tom.

"Like hell you don't!" snarled Spider Stokes, glaring hatred through red-rimmed eyes.

Tom spotted Scar at the edge of the crowd. "I told you I'd fight my own battles," he yelled.

The big man held up two bear-like hands, nodding his scarred head to his left. Tom followed his eyes. Mary Read stood slightly apart from the rest of the crowd, a cutlass in her belt and a pistol in her hand. Tom gaped at her then back at the scowling pirates.

"Got a woman to fight for you, did you?" sneered Spider. "I've met some cowards in my time, but nothing as low as you."

The mob growled their agreement. A few spat at Tom but most just stared with down-turned mouths, narrowed eyes and shaking heads. He flinched under their combined glare. "I didn't know," he pleaded. "I came here to fight."

"Yeah," spat Spider. "To fight a corpse. Very brave of you."

"I… I…" Tom stuttered to a stop. After a few seconds he spun on his heel and hurried away from his accusers, head hanging on stooped shoulders.

CHAPTER 7

MUTINY

The pirates quickly went back to getting drunk on stolen rum. They swilled it down by the jugful and were soon singing, laughing and arguing, Ben Sloane's body lying forgotten in a hastily dug grave.

Dan found Tom, head in hands, slumped under a coconut tree by the edge of the beach. "Are you alright mate," he asked, though he already knew the answer.

"No," said Tom. "I'm not alright."

Dan looked up to the top of the tree. It must have been fifty feet tall. "I wouldn't sit there, if I were you. A coconut could kill you, falling from that height."

"To be honest Dan, I don't really care."

"Don't talk daft. It's not that bad."

"Isn't it?" Tom brought his knees up to his chest and hugged them to him. "How can I face my friends after that? They despise me."

"Your friends don't despise you, Tom. Those people aren't your friends. They're thieves and murderers. What they think shouldn't matter to you."

"Well it does," moaned Tom, his head still bowed.

"They may not be your friends but they are mine. They *were* mine."

Dan sighed. "Now is when you'll find out who your real friends are. Scar and me, we'll stick by you. And Mary."

"Don't mention her name," snapped Tom. "She's ruined my life!"

"She saved your life, Tom. Ben Sloane would have killed you."

"I may as well be dead."

Dan could think of nothing else to say. He looked up at the coconuts again. "Do you mind if I move away from the tree?"

"Suit yourself," said Tom, picking up a small stick and scratching random lines in the sand. "You can keep on moving if you want. I'd rather be on my own."

Dan said nothing but sat down a few yards away.

Tom spotted Mary Read making her way up the beach. "Oh no," he groaned. "That's all I need." He lowered his head again and hugged his knees.

Mary stood over him silently for a minute. Tom didn't look up.

"Sorry Tom," she said at last, "but he would have killed you."

"What's it to you," snapped Tom.

"I like you. Why should I let a bilge-rat like that kill a decent man?"

Tom raised his head and his voice. "It was a duel. A matter of honour."

"Honour?" said Mary sharply, her hands on her hips.

"Don't think there was a scrap of honour in Ben Sloane, because there wasn't."

Tom looked away but Mary went on. "And it wasn't a duel, it would have been murder. Sloane knew he could beat you. That's why he agreed to fight."

Tom scowled. "He fought *you* didn't he?"

"I'm just a woman. He thought he could beat me easily. But he didn't know me. He made a big mistake."

Tom stared sullenly at his feet.

"I was telling the truth when I said I'd been in the army," she went on. "I joined up disguised as a man. Served my time in Holland in the late wars. Ben Sloane might have had a chance with a cutlass on a swaying deck, but with pistol or musket on dry land? I can out-shoot any sailor."

"So you knew you could beat him?"

"Yes," replied Mary.

"So you're a murderer," said Tom churlishly.

"I may be," admitted Mary, unfazed by Tom's tone. "But *that* wasn't murder. I just exterminated a piece of vermin that was infesting the ship."

"You're a murderer!"

Mary's eyes narrowed. "You shouldn't push me away, Tom. You don't have many friends as it is."

"No I don't," Tom shouted. "Thanks to you!"

Mary Read held her arms up in surrender. "I'll see you later, when you've calmed down a bit."

"Not if I see you first," said Tom, his face red. "You've ruined my life."

Mary shook her head and walked away.

"Tom!" Urgency rang through Dan's voice, but Tom didn't look up. "Tom!"

He shook his friend by the shoulder, but Tom shrugged him off. "Leave me alone. I just want to be on my own."

Dan wasn't listening. "Tom, look!"

Tom slowly raised his head. Behind Dan's frantically waving arm he could see three ships ghosting into the bay, their gun-ports opening and black muzzles suddenly appearing as unseen crewmen ran the cannons out, ready to fire.

Tom looked to his right. The pirates were huddled together drinking rum, oblivious to the danger. He jumped to his feet. "We've got to warn the others!"

He set off at a run, shouting and hollering, with Dan close behind him. Before they reached the pirates, a huge roar hammered their eardrums as the leading ship fired its broadside. The pirates' boats, left above the waterline when they came ashore, disappeared in a shower of wood and splinters. A moment of total silence descended on the beach then pandemonium broke out as the yelling pirates sprinted for the tree-line.

The second ship fired its broadside into the forest. Splinters flew in all directions and a shower of coconuts and broken branches rained down on the pirates, knocking two unconscious. The rest panicked and ran back out onto the beach again. They milled around in a confused mass as one of the strange ships pulled alongside the *Kingston*.

Armed men poured over the side and onto the captured merchantman. The pirates watched helplessly from the shore as the boarders hunted their hung-over friends through the ship and dragged them out onto the deck. They quickly bound them before placing nooses around their straining necks. Cheering sailors, released from the hold, grabbed the ropes and gleefully ran the kicking, choking pirates up to the yardarm.

Patrick Carty raised his musket but Calico Jack pushed the barrel down. "They're out of range. There's nothing we can do."

The stranded pirates on shore cursed in impotent rage.

"Animals," yelled McKaig. "We let them live and how dae they repay us?"

Beside him, Noah Harwood spat into the sand, his eyes fixed on the kicking bodies swinging from the masts.

Neither was any mercy shown to the pirates found on the *William*. The boarders hauled them high into the rigging by their necks. Arms tied behind their backs, they danced out the gallows' jig.

A few pirates, startled out of drunken slumbers by the thunder of the guns, managed to jump overboard and struck out for the beach. The shore-party cheered them on but musket fire from the ships cut them down until only one remained. It was the Welshman, Gareth Griffiths. All the marksmen now concentrated on him. The men on shore screamed encouragement as he swam on, spouts of water jumping all around him as the muskets coughed death. Suddenly he half-leapt out of the water as a heavy musket ball hit him in the back, then another. The cheering died in the pirates' throats, and they looked on in horrified silence as, arms flailing, he sank beneath the blood-reddening waves.

The bounty-hunters put a skeleton crew on the *William* and a token force in charge of the *Kingston*, which they left to be manned by its own seamen. Without waiting to cut down the hanged men, they got under way. The pirates looked on in helpless fury as their ships, following after two of the raiders, sailed silently out of the bay with their comrade's bodies swinging lifeless in the rigging. The third raider turned broadside onto the beach.

"Down!" yelled Calico Jack and the pirates hurled themselves to the ground as the guns erupted. Sand lashed into Dan's face as a round shot hit the beach in front of him and bounced harmlessly over his head. One man screamed briefly as a cannonball plucked him from the ground and threw his twitching body back to the tree-line. Then there was silence apart from the slapping of the closing gun-ports and the snapping of sails as the ship came about, beam onto the wind, and glided out of the bay.

The sullen pirates gathered around Calico Jack. "This is your fault" snarled Spider Stokes. "We shouldn't have chanced our arm so close to Port Royal. It was asking for trouble."

"You voted for it," snapped Jack. "We're a democratic company and you voted for it."

"And you're captain. You're supposed to give us good advice." Spider turned to the other pirates. "I say we vote him out. What say you?"

"Aye!" went up a loud shout.

George Featherston called out above the hubbub. "Who'll navigate? You need Jack Rackham."

"Why do we need a navigator?" sneered Spider. "We haven't got a ship, thanks to him. Anyway, you can navigate?"

"I'm with the captain," said George and strode over to stand by his side.

"Me too!" cried Anne Bonny as she and Mary Read moved to flank Jack.

Calico Jack drew himself up to his full height. "I can get us off this island," he called to the wavering mob. His cutlass flashed out and quivered an inch from Spider's gulping throat. "Do you think this little runt can? He's all mouth and trousers."

The men hesitated.

"Who's with me?" shouted the captain.

Noah Harwood stepped across and placed himself at Jack's back.

"I dinnae ken why I'm joining ye," moaned McKaig as he limped over. "Yer a terrible captain. At least we had a ship when I signed on. I'm no good at sailing on dry land – no' wi' this leg."

"Aye, ye're useless," agreed Thackeray as he joined McKaig.

"Welcome aboard gentlemen," smiled Jack.

"I'm with you," said Richard Corner the quartermaster, joining the small band around the captain.

James Dobbin and Patrick Carty, both seasoned topmen, made their way over with the gunner, John Davis, and the sailmaker, Thomas Earl. Thomas Bourn and Old Dad Fenwick hesitated then threw their lot in with Calico Jack.

Spider Stokes sensed the situation slipping away from

him. His face red, he raised his reedy voice. "You can't stick with him. He's no good. We set out to make our fortunes, and now we've got nothing. No ship, no loot, no women — nothing! He has to go!"

Many of the men growled their agreement.

John Howell, the carpenter who'd reluctantly volunteered when the pirates had taken his ship, dithered between the two hostile groups. His bolt-upright, ginger hair looked even more terrified than he did. He took his choice, the lesser of two evils. His mind made up, his worried face uncreased and even his hair seemed to relax a little as he joined Calico Jack.

Tom placed himself at the captain's side. "Come on Dan," he called.

Dan hesitated. In his heart he knew where his loyalties lay, but he thought it unlikely that Jack would be going anywhere near Jamaica - and that's where he needed to be if he was ever to find his dad.

Scar noticed his indecision. "Jack best chance, Dan. This rabble starve or be taken and hanged. Unless cut each other throat first. Choice is live or die. Jack only choice." Dan followed Scar as he strode over to the smaller group.

"Anyone else?" called Calico Jack. "Last chance!"

No one moved.

"Alright," said Jack. "We'll just be taking our fair share of the food and water, then we'll be on our way."

"You'll not be taking anything," snarled Spider Stokes. "You're lucky we're letting you leave with your lives."

Anne Bonny and Mary Read jumped forward, pulling out their pistols and putting them to Spider's head. The small man went white and what little chin he had visibly trembled, his eyes blinking rapidly at the levelled pistols. Jack's men's cutlasses rasped from their belts. Although outnumbered five to one, they stood resolute and the mob, leaderless now that Spider had lost his tongue, moved aside as those loyal to Jack pushed forward and filled knapsacks with water bottles and scraps of food.

"Leave the rum!" Jack shouted as McKaig held his canteen to a rum barrel. "We stay sober until we're out of this mess. Come on. Let's go!"

"Rum's the only decent thing we've captured since we set sail and now we have tae leave it. Some, bleedin' captain!" grumbled McKaig, but he followed Jack as he led his small group up the beach away from their one-time comrades. The others watched them sullenly before turning back to the rum barrels.

They had trudged along the sand for a mile, each deep in his own thoughts, when they came to a gap in the jungle beside the beach. The path led inland.

"There's a port on the other side of the island where we can steal a ship," said Jack. "We can either carry on right around the island or we can cut across here. It's up to you. The path should be a lot quicker but it means going through the jungle."

"Well I'm fed up stumbling through this sand," said McKaig. "I'm in it up to my stump every other step. I say we cut across."

"I don't know," said George Featherston. "It's a risk and our luck isn't good at the moment."

As he spoke, a scream rent the air, then another and

another. They spun around, eyes darting back the way they'd come. Men lay on the ground, arrows protruding from their twitching bodies. The rest of the pirates ran here and there, a leaderless rabble.

A huge whoop carried up the beach and native warriors poured out of the jungle, battering at the stunned pirates with tomahawks and war clubs. They fought back in knots of two or three, but there was no unity and each little fighting group soon fell under the bludgeoning weapons of their attackers.

"Quick," yelled Jack. "Off the beach!"

Tom hesitated, moving back towards his one-time shipmates.

Scar grabbed him by the arm. "Can't save them," he growled. "Just pray we save ourselves." He dragged Tom from the beach to the path where the rest of Jack's band were already running for their lives.

They stopped their headlong flight a couple of miles from the beach and threw themselves to the ground, gasping for breath.

"Do you think they saw us?" rasped Dan, his heaving chest dragging in painful lungful's of hot, humid air.

"They saw us," said Calico Jack. "They waited till the two groups split up before they attacked. They were probably watching all morning hoping we'd kill each other and save them the job."

"Hadn't we better get off the path then," put in George Featherston, darting a glance back the way they'd come. All he saw was McKaig and Thackeray still stumbling up the path as fast as they could manage.

"No point," said Jack. "They're Caribs. They know this jungle better than us. They'd hunt us down. Speed is our best chance. So we stick to the path."

McKaig and Thackeray caught up with them, hanging on to each other, their chests heaving.

"Thackeray's too slow," croaked McKaig. "We should... leave him behind. He'll... hold us up."

"Shut yer bone-box, McKaig. I got here... before you," gasped Thackeray.

"That's coz I was... helping ye along... useless old tortoise that ye are."

"I may be old... but I'm still faster than you and yer tree-stump!"

"Save your breath, the pair of you," said Calico Jack. "You'll be needing it. We'll be off again in five minutes."

McKaig and Thackeray sank down, back to back.

Calico Jack took off his tricorn hat and dusted it down with his other hand. "We can only hope our old shipmates put up a good fight, and those savages take their time killing and looting before they come after us. If they discover the rum then we've got a chance. If not? Then we run, and the Devil take the hindmost."

"Thackeray, ye mean?" said McKaig.

"Ye'll be in hell before me, McKaig," snapped Thackeray as he clambered to his feet and stumbled on up the path.

"I'll save ye a nice warm spot if I am," called McKaig, limping after him.

The small band set off after the two old pirates.

CHAPTER 8

CANNIBALS

A chill had fallen with the night. The small band of pirates huddled together, hidden in the jungle at the side of the path. They dared not light a fire for fear of giving away their position to the Caribs. Most of the pirates had fallen into an exhausted sleep. They were fit and strong from a lifetime of toil on the high seas but, confined as they normally were to the small wooden world of a ship, they were not used to running any distance.

Dan leant back against a tree, Scar at his side. Tired as he was, he couldn't sleep as he listened to the sound of strange animals prowling through the jungle, punctuated by the occasional primal scream as a predator caught its prey. Dan realised that he had become used to being the predator. The thought that he was now the prey sent a shiver through him.

He glanced over at the huge man beside him. Scar was awake. Dan felt an overwhelming need to talk, though Jack had urged them to silence. "Scar," he whispered. The big man grunted. "Can I ask you something?" Another grunt. "Where did you come from before you were captured? Before you became a slave?"

"Was born slave," said Scar, pain etched in his voice.

Dan stared at him, trying to make out his features in the darkness. "You were born a slave? You've never known freedom?"

"Have known freedom. Was free on pirate ship, and free is how Scar stay!"

A steely edge had crept into Scar's voice and Dan knew he should leave the conversation, but he couldn't help himself. "Have you got any family," he asked and immediately regretted it. Scar had been at sea for over ten years and had probably put any thoughts of his family behind him long ago.

It was a few minutes before Scar spoke again. "Mother was Ashanti from Africa." He stirred in the darkness, looking intently at Dan. "Father was Irish."

Dan stared at him, open-mouthed. "You're Irish?"

"Never seen Ireland. Never seen Africa." Scar shifted his body heavily in the thick undergrowth. "Parents both warriors. Mother fought for Ashanti against the Fante. They capture her and sell to slavers. Ship to Jamaica." He paused for a few moments then went on. "Father fought for Catholic tribe against English at Boyne River in Ireland. They capture and sell as slave. Him and all his warriors."

Dan gaped at Scar through the gloom. He was vaguely aware that thousands of Irish had been shipped to the colonies under Cromwell and again after the Glorious Revolution, but he'd never really considered their fate. "Are your parents still alive?" he asked.

"Father strong man but Jamaica sun stronger. Collapse in fields and they leave him there. I six years old when he die."

Dan felt a surge of sympathy. He'd been six when he'd lost *his* father to the press-gang.

Scar went on. "Mother take me and escape, but they catch and cut off foot so she not run again. Leg go bad. She die."

"Scar, I…" He tailed off as the big man turned away and Dan didn't press him further. He went back to listening to the disembodied sounds of the jungle and drifted into a fitful sleep.

Dan dreamt he was back on the *Dover*. The sadistic bosun had beaten him with a knotted rope and was now slowly choking him to death. He started awake, his eyes bulging, a scream stifled by a large hand clamped over his mouth. He recognised Scar in the half-light of early dawn. The big man held a finger to his lips then moved on to wake the next man.

A twig snapped and Dan's head jerked around. He froze. Through the trees he could see a long file of Caribs jogging along the path. Out of the shade of the jungle, the early morning sun shone on the bright feathers in their oiled hair. They were so close he could make out necklaces of teeth bouncing off their muscular chests as they ran, and he gave an involuntary shudder. He held his breath but his heart slammed so hard against his ribcage he was sure they would hear him.

Finally the last of the warriors passed by, and Dan's

breathing slowly returned to normal. The pirates gathered around Calico Jack as he beckoned them to him.

"What now?" asked George Featherston.

"We wait until nightfall then we move on under cover of darkness."

The bosun frowned. "What if they're camped out on the path for the night? What if we stumble into them?"

"Have you got a better idea?"

"Yes! We should turn back."

"Back to what? If we go by the beach they can track us easily in the sand. They've probably sent another war-party that way anyhow." Calico Jack rubbed the stubble on his usually well-scraped chin. "We keep to the path and travel by night. We move slowly and watch our step. Any strange noise, and we hide in the jungle."

The bosun remained unconvinced but the rest of the pirates agreed with Jack's plan. None of them were keen to leave the shelter of the jungle as the day brightened around them.

The time passed slowly. Dan jumped at every sound, his nerves stretched tighter than the skin on a drum. Jack came over and leant back against the tree next to him. "Are you alright, Dan?" he asked quietly.

"I'm fine," Dan lied, sweat streaking his face in the humid jungle air.

"Try and get some sleep then. We've a long night ahead of us."

Dan regarded the pirate captain as he closed his eyes and pulled his hat down over his face. He didn't seem to have a care in the world. "There was one thing I wanted to ask."

Calico Jack sighed and tilted his hat back up, looking tolerantly at Dan.

"It was those Indians," said Dan, wiping sweat from his eyes. "Their necklaces. They looked like they were made of human teeth."

"Well that would be no surprise. They're cannibals."

Despite the heat a cold shiver ran up Dan's spine. "Cannibals?"

Other pirates began to gather around, faces white.

"And when exactly were ye gonnae tell us this?" McKaig butted in.

"It's common knowledge," said Calico Jack. "They're Carib tribesmen. The word 'cannibal' comes from the name 'Carib'."

"Is that why they're after us?" asked Dan. "Are they hungry?"

Calico Jack stifled a laugh. "No Dan. They're not hungry, but they've no love for white men. They used to dominate the Caribbean, hence the name, but the Spanish drove them out of the main islands. Killed them with muskets and smallpox, or took them as slaves for the silver mines on the mainland."

Scar stood over them. "Took them slave?" he repeated. "Don't blame them for try to kill us."

"They were slavers themselves once," said Jack looking up into Scar's angry face. "The original people in these islands were the Taino. The word means 'peace', but they got precious little of that from the Caribs. They raided their villages, killed and ate the men, raped the women and castrated the boys before taking them for slaves."

Dan gulped and crossed his legs.

"Aye," said Jack, warming to his story now he had an audience. "The Caribs are a bloodthirsty lot. They were the original pirates of the Caribbean. They'd hunt down Spanish merchant ships in hundred man war-canoes. Showed them no mercy. They got fat on Spanish sailors."

The pirates were horrified now. Jack smiled. "Their favourite are Frenchmen. They'll go out of their way to make a meal of a Frenchman. They say the Spanish are edible, but a bit stringy. You don't need to worry though. They don't like Englishmen. They say we taste awful."

"But I'm Irish," gulped Dan.

"Don't worry. They don't eat boys. They just..." Jack made a snipping motion with his fingers.

Dan shuddered and re-crossed his legs.

"McKaig's not English," Thackeray grinned.

"If they catch us, let's hope they get Thackeray first" snapped the Scotsman. "They'll be feasting on him for a month before they'll bother with the rest of us."

When the pirates fell quiet again, Jack dropped in his final snippet of information. "They paint themselves red when they plan to take no prisoners."

"They're painted red now," gasped Dan. "I saw them."

"We'd best not get caught then," said Jack. "So keep the noise down, get some rest, and do what I tell you, when I tell you."

With that he pulled his hat back down over his eyes, and nodded off.

After snatching what sleep they could, they set off up the

path as night fell. They stumbled along, stopping and listening intently whenever they heard any strange noise. Each bend in the path set their hearts racing as they wondered if the Caribs were waiting around the corner.

As the night drew on they became weary but kept plodding along the cleared path, jungle towering above them on either side. Calico Jack suddenly stopped and the pirates bumped into each other in the dark, swearing and muttering. Dan peered through the trees where the path bent around ahead of them, and thought he could make out the flicker of flames.

"I need two volunteers to check what that is," whispered Jack.

"It's bleedin' obvious what it is," growled McKaig. "It's bleedin' Injuns, that's what it is!"

"Keep your voice down," hissed Jack. "Two volunteers?"

"We'll go," Tom piped up. "Come on Dan!"

"What do you mean, 'come on Dan'? I don't remember volunteering."

Tom crept off up the path. Dan sighed and followed him into the darkness.

As they neared the bend, Tom stopped and waited for Dan to catch up. "We'll cut through the jungle," he whispered. "Spy out the land from the cover of the trees."

There was a rustling sound as Tom disappeared into the bushes.

Dan took a deep breath then followed his friend into the thick undergrowth. Something touched his arm and he jumped, only just stifling a scream.

"You thought I was something nasty, didn't you?" chuckled Tom.

"You *are* something nasty," hissed Dan. "You nearly gave me a heart attack."

"Okay! Don't fill your pants. Indians have a good sense of smell."

"Keep your voice down," urged Dan. "You've got a whisper like a fog-horn."

"Alright. Hold onto my shirt-tails and follow me."

They made their way stealthily towards the flickering light. When they arrived at the jungle's edge they could see a number of fires burning low. Around them, fast asleep, lay dozens of Carib warriors. Dan could smell rum and noticed drinking vessels strewn about. Tom stared in a trance. Dan pulled at his arm, and they crept back the way they had come.

Calico Jack rubbed his chin thoughtfully. "You say there were no sentries?"

"We didn't see any," said Tom.

"And they'd been drinking?"

"I could smell rum," said Dan. "And they were sprawled everywhere. I'd say they're drunk."

Calico Jack looked hard at him. "Would you stake your life on it?"

Dan gulped. "Ehmm..."

Jack smiled grimly. "Well *I'm* going to stake your life on it. All of our lives." He turned to the others. "Make sure your muskets and pistols are primed."

"You've lost your mind," gasped Thackeray. "We can't

attack a hundred men with just seventeen!"

"Eighteen!" piped up McKaig.

"I'm not counting you," said Thackeray. "You can hardly lift a musket, never mind fire one."

"I can out-shoot you, ye useless piece of–"

"Shut it," hissed Calico Jack. "We're not going to attack them. They're drunk, and we're going to creep through them while they sleep it off."

"You're mad," snapped Thackeray. "Why don't we cut through the jungle?"

Jack pulled a face. "Seventeen of us, stumbling through the jungle in the dark? I don't think so."

"Eighteen," spluttered McKaig.

Jack went on. "The noise would wake them for sure. And we'd get split up and lost. They'd hunt us down one by one and butcher us."

"Can't we just wait?" asked George Featherston. "Stay hidden?"

"We've no food left and precious little water. We have to keep moving. And they're between us and the port. This is our chance to get ahead of them again. They're in a drunken stupor. This is our best chance."

Jack paused, waiting for more arguments, but none came. "We need complete silence," he said. "And that includes you McKaig. If you open that big mouth of yours we're all going to die."

"We're all gonna die then," groaned Thackeray.

The Scotsman glared at him but said nothing.

Calico Jack set off, with the small band at his heels. They reached the bend and the captain peered cautiously around it. He could see sleeping warriors but no sentries. He waved Dan and Tom to the front as they had already checked out the Carib camp.

The night was cool but Dan could feel the sweat trickling down his back as he stepped out into the firelight with Tom at his side. No challenge came from the sleeping camp. They moved closer, creeping slowly along until they were in amongst the Carib war-party. Dan could hear his ragged breath rasping in his lungs as his chest heaved up and down, and he tried but failed to breathe more quietly. Still no-one stirred. They carried on, moving painfully slowly, one careful footstep after another, trying to avoid twigs, discarded drinking vessels and sprawled bodies.

After what seemed like a lifetime, the last campfire slid slowly past. Tom winked at Dan in the flickering half-light of the fires. 'Piece of cake,' he mouthed. They looked back at the others who were now inching towards them.

Then McKaig found his tongue. "We should butcher them all while they're asleep." His rasping whisper seemed to reverberate around the camp.

Everyone froze. Two nearby Caribs stirred and rolled over. The pirates, standing like statues, willed them to sleep on. McKaig's burst of bravado had deserted him and he glanced around, eyes wide in the firelight. The two warriors settled back down and lay still. The pirates crept over to where Dan and Tom waited, then they all ghosted on in silence until the Carib camp was a dull glow behind them.

Calico Jack rounded on the Scotsman. "You're a fool,

McKaig! What the hell do you think you were doing? I said, total silence!"

"I told you he'd not be able to do it," growled Thackeray. "His mouth's ten times the size of his brain."

"We could ha' done it," McKaig argued stubbornly. "They were all pished. We could ha' slaughtered them in their sleep, then we wouldnae have tae keep lookin' o'er our shoulders and waiting for an arrow in the back."

George Featherston stepped towards him, his big fists clenched, but Calico Jack held up his hand and sighed. "What's done is done. Come on. Let's put some distance between us and them before daybreak."

With a final glare at McKaig, the bosun turned and hurried off along the path with the others following as fast as they dared in the dull light of the moon.

CHAPTER 9

DELIVERANCE

Dawn came at last. The bosun urged Jack to let the men sleep, but he was determined to keep going. A few remarks about cannibalism proved persuasive and they stumbled on, mile after weary mile.

No-one talked now. They were too tired. Even McKaig had gone quiet as he limped along supporting himself on Thackeray's stout shoulder.

"Look!" Tom bounced up and down as he pointed up the path towards the westering sun.

Dan peered ahead and thought he could make out a glimmer of blue.

"It's the sea," cried Tom. "We've made it!"

Before Calico Jack could stop them, the small band let out a cheer. "The Caribs could be close behind," he exploded. "If they didn't know where we are, they do now!"

As if in answer to his words a great 'whoop' cut the humid air. Dan felt a chill bite through him.

"Run," shouted Jack, and they made off as fast as they could on tired legs. "I reckon they're half a mile behind," he cried. "We can still make it!"

Fear and adrenalin carried them on, and they increased the pace despite their exhaustion. But McKaig was falling behind.

"Get on my back," panted Thackeray. "I'll carry you."

"You get on *my* back!"

"Stop arguing and get on my back, blast yer eyes! Ye'll get us both killed!"

McKaig opened his mouth to speak but any argument was cut short as Scar plucked him from his feet, and jogged off with him over his shoulder. Thackeray lumbered on, grinning despite his aching lungs and the danger behind.

They plunged on along the path. Dan could hear the war whoops, closer now. They broke out of the jungle and his spirits rose. Ahead he could see a gated wall guarding a small harbour town. But there was still half a mile to go, and they were slowing as tired legs rebelled against the cruel pace being set.

Dan glanced back as the Carib war-party burst from the trees. A blood-curdling scream erupted as they spotted their prey and broke into a sprint.

Dan willed his tired legs to go faster, but they refused. The gate loomed close now but the leading Carib warriors charged ever nearer. Dan imagined he could feel their fetid breath on the back of his neck and an involuntary moan escaped his lips. His legs finally obeyed him and sped up.

The pirates were strung out now, with Thackeray struggling at the rear. They'd almost reached the gate and voices on the walls urged them on in their deadly race.

Then Thackeray sank to his knees. "I can't go on," he

rasped. "Leave me!"

"Put me down," bellowed McKaig, and Scar lowered him to the ground. The Scotsman pulled a brace of pistols from his belt and stumbled back towards Thackeray, screaming curses at the Caribs and his shipmate.

The first warrior reached Thackeray. With a wild yell he brought his war club high above his head. McKaig fired a pistol and the shot plucked the man from his feet. Another Carib loomed over him and the Scotsman put a bullet in his brain. He threw down his empty pistols and grabbed Thackeray by the collar. "Come on, ye son of a bachelor. On yer feet!" He began to drag the protesting old pirate back towards the gates, but the main body of Caribs was nearly on them.

"Leave me, ye fool," shouted Thackeray struggling in his grasp. "Get away! Save yerself!"

McKaig let go, and placed himself between his friend and the advancing war-party. "Come on ye heathens," he yelled, waving his cutlass. "Come and chew on this!"

With a great effort of will, Thackeray struggled to his feet and planted himself beside McKaig, sword in hand.

Tom and the bosun had seen enough. They drew their pistols and ran back towards the two old pirates. Scar started off after them with Dan close behind.

"Hell's teeth!" cursed Calico Jack, nearly at the safety of the gate. He looked in dismay at the small band of brothers hurrying back the way they'd come. He made his decision. Screaming a war-cry of his own he led the rest of the pirates after the others.

McKaig and Thackeray were hacking desperately at

their tormentors as the rest of the crew reached them and discharged their fire-arms at point-blank range. The leading warriors were hurled from their feet in a squall of blood and screams. The rest hesitated then came on, slowly but inexorably. Dan couldn't take his eyes from the necklaces of human teeth bouncing on the red-painted chests of the Caribs as they closed in.

The pirates drew their cutlasses and waited to die.

The screaming tribesmen were nearly on them. Dan stood beside Tom, gripping his knife tightly. His earlier fears had evaporated and a strange calm had settled on him. The advancing warriors seemed to be coming on at a crawl as if time itself had slowed down. He glanced at his friend and felt a pang of regret that he'd got him into this, and another that he would never get to see his father again.

Dan turned back to face the Caribs and, as he raised his knife, he heard a bellow of defiance. With a shock he realised that the sound was coming from him. The other pirates took up the shout and roared out their own challenge.

"Abajo! Abajo!" came a call from behind.

"Get down!" screamed Calico Jack, and they threw themselves to the earth.

McKaig alone stood his ground. "I'm gonnae die on my feet," he yelled.

"Foot!" growled Thackeray as he dragged him down, just in time.

"Fuego!" shouted the voice, and a great roar split the air. The front rank of Carib warriors was flung backwards as a volley of musket balls hammered into them.

"Fuego!" came the voice again.

A second volley ripped into the tribesmen and the survivors shuddered to a halt, those at the rear already drifting back up the path. The distinct clank of metal on metal made Dan look behind. The Spanish garrison had sallied out and they were now fixing bayonets.

"Atacar!"

Spanish soldiers, steel-tipped muskets levelled, charged past, and the Caribs turned and fled.

The pirates looked around, barely believing what had happened. Tom caught Dan's eye. "We're alive!" he yelled. "Dan, we're alive!" They hugged each other and bounced up and down laughing and shouting. Some of the pirates joined in, dancing mad jigs of joy. Others collapsed to the ground letting relief claim their last dregs of energy.

"On your feet!" yelled Calico Jack. "Reload your weapons!"

"Have a heart Jack," croaked George Featherston. "They're exhausted. Let them rest."

"This isn't a friendly town," cried Jack. "It's Spanish, and Spain is at war with Britain. When they find out who we are we'll be hanged as spies or pirates."

He paused to let that sink in. "This is our chance! The garrison is off chasing the Caribs. We can seize a ship. One last effort. That's all I ask."

The pirates slowly dragged themselves to their feet and, with shaking hands, began to load muskets and pistols.

"Now, let's get into the town before the garrison gets back," said Jack, marching towards the gates. Dan and the others filed after him.

A single sentry challenged them. Calico Jack answered in Spanish but the guard raised his voice and his musket. Mary Read slipped a knife between his ribs, searching out his heart. The Spaniard sank to the ground with no more than a sigh.

Dan stared at the bloody knife in horror. "They saved us," he yelled. "They just saved us!"

"And I just saved us again," said Mary, wiping her knife on the dead man's coat. "We've no time to argue. We have to seize a ship and get out of here fast."

"She's right, Dan," said Calico Jack, but his lip curled in distaste as he regarded the blood-stained woman. "We're definitely dead if they catch us now."

They made their way down to the dock as quickly as their aching legs allowed. Jack stood at the waterfront and scanned the ships in the harbour with a practised eye. "That one!" he said, pointing out a single-masted sloop. "She's small enough to sail with a crew of seventeen."

"Eighteen!" croaked McKaig.

"And she's big enough to sail the high seas." Jack's eyes roamed around the quay. Two rowing boats bobbed at the water's edge. An old man in the stern of the nearest looked up. Jack pointed out the sloop.

"Cinco," said the white-haired man, holding out a calloused hand. Jack pointed his pistol at the man's head, and the pirates clambered into the two boats and began rowing out to the sloop. At the tiller of the first, the old man muttered and cursed but brought them to the ship they were after.

As they drew near, Dan could see she was called *Santa Anna*. He scanned the deck for any sign of life but saw none. The boats scraped against the hull and the pirates clambered up the side. They quickly ran through the ship but there was nobody aboard.

Calico Jack strode onto the quarterdeck. "Tom, Dobbin, Bourn, Patrick. Get the canvas up."

With tired arms, they slowly hoisted the sail.

"Damn and blast," swore Calico Jack as he studied the mast. A large crack ran down its entire length. "I knew this was too good to be true. She'll not take a full spread of canvas. Reef the mainsail!"

He stroked his chin as he thought. "Scar! Take Dan and check the stern-chaser. Make sure it's loaded. We can't outrun them if they give chase — not with this mast. We'll have to fight our way out." He paced around shouting orders, showing no sign of fatigue. "The rest of you get to the capstan. Up anchor!"

Dan and Scar made their way to the back of the quarterdeck. The cannon wasn't loaded. They hurried below, found the magazine, and Scar snapped the padlock from the door. Back on deck they quickly charged and primed the cannon.

Angry cries of alarm came from the shore. Dan could see lines of men shouting and pointing at the departing ship. He guessed the murdered sentry had been found. They'd be chased for sure, but hopefully not until the garrison returned.

"Scar," called Calico Jack. "Send a shot into them. Make them think twice about trying to board us."

Dan stared in disbelief. "But they saved us. We can't fire at them!"

"Just do it!" yelled Calico Jack.

Scar took Dan by the arm and pulled him to the stern. "We aim at boats, not men," he growled.

The round shot smashed into the quayside, missing the men but causing them to scatter.

"More powder," called Scar, and Dan dashed off, quickly falling into the old familiar pattern he'd learnt aboard the *Dover*.

"Galleons!" came a sudden shout of alarm. "Spanish galleons!"

Dan hurried back out into the fast-fading light of dusk. He stopped and gaped in horror. Two ships blocked the harbour entrance; a sloop and a big, sixty-four-gun man-o-war, with the proud red and white flag of Spain flying from her mizzen mast.

They were trapped.

CHAPTER 10

THE SPANISH GALLEON

Bottled up in the harbour, they dropped anchor and lowered the sails. They looked on helplessly as townsmen rowed out to the galleon, doubtless telling them that pirates had taken *Santa Anna*. Dan squinted at the harbour entrance. He could still make out the shapes of the Spanish warships, as the sun dipped under the horizon. "What are they waiting for?" he groaned. "Why don't they come in and finish us?"

"The water's too shallow for the galleon," said the bosun.

"For the moment," Thackeray added gloomily.

"The sloop's small enough to get in," guessed Dan.

"Why risk her?" The bosun studied the high-water mark on the harbour wall. "We're not going anywhere, and they know it. They'll wait for morning. Come high tide that galleon will sail in and blast us all to hell."

Thackeray scowled. "We're wasting time then? We should be on shore, making a run for it."

Behind them, McKaig groaned. "I dinnae want tae go through that again. We should find a tavern, spend the night with a woman and a bottle, and then die happy on the morrow."

"They'd slit our throats ashore for what we've done," said the bosun. "And anyway, Jack's got a plan." But there was nothing but doubt in his tired voice.

The small company gathered on deck, waiting for the captain to speak. An air of doom hung over the ship and the crew stood in cloying silence.

Calico Jack faced them from the quarterdeck. "This is a bit of luck," he said cheerfully. "Now we don't need to break our backs putting in a new mast."

The pirates stared at him open-mouthed.

"Aye, coz we'll all be dead," shouted McKaig. "That's a great comfort that is."

Jack smiled. "We don't need to repair *Santa Anna,* because the Spaniards have been kind enough to bring us a nice English-built sloop to replace her."

"Somehow I dinnae think they'll want tae swap," muttered the Scotsman.

Calico Jack looked over to the harbour entrance where the Spanish ships were still visible against the darkening sky. He turned back to the dejected pirates. "What do you make of that sloop, George? Would you say she's a captured prize?"

"Aye, she's a British ship, right enough," said the bosun gruffly. "If *she* couldn't fight off the galleon, what chance have *we* got?"

"So there'll only be a few Spaniards on board as a prize crew," said the captain. "And a couple of dozen Englishmen locked in the hold, no doubt."

"Aye, Jack!" The bosun's tone brightened. "You're right!"

The rest of the crew frowned at each other in puzzlement.

Jack paced up and down, animated now. "Make sure your knives and cutlasses are sharp, but keep your pistols in your belts. We have to do this quietly."

"Do what?" asked Dan.

"In the morning, that Spanish galleon is going to sail in and blow *Santa Anna* to pieces."

"But at least our knives will be sharp," groaned McKaig.

"But we'll not be aboard *Santa Anna*," smiled the captain. "We'll be on that Spanish prize." He paused to let this sink in. "We take the sloop in the night and then, come morning when that galleon sails in and starts to pound *Santa Anna*, we slip away. She'll be so busy making sure of her kill she won't even notice us going. When they do realise what's happened, they still have to turn that big clumsy tub around in this small harbour. We'll be long gone by then."

A murmur of excitement ran through the ship as condemned men suddenly saw a glimmer of hope.

"It could work," said McKaig, his spirits rising. "It could work."

"It *will* work," cried Jack. "As long as we keep total silence."

Thackeray glared at McKaig. "It's not going to work then," he muttered.

Tom spoke up. "If we capture the sloop, why don't we

just escape in the night? Put some distance between us and the galleon before daylight."

"Because they'd notice if we put up the canvas tonight," said Jack. "We'd never make it. In the morning they'll be expecting the sloop's sails to go up, and then they'll be too busy battering *Santa Anna* to notice we've gone."

"Jack's right," said George Featherston. "If we take the sloop quietly, then bide our time until daybreak, we can do this."

Dan could almost physically feel the buzz of excitement in the ship.

"Needles," called Calico Jack. They all knew Thomas Earl, the sailmaker, as 'Needles'. "Sew me up a flag. White skull over crossed swords on a black background. Come the morning, I want them to see for certain that we're a pirate ship. We don't want them sending in a boat to make sure. If they board and find *Santa Anna* empty, then we've had it."

When the flag was ready, they hoisted it to the top of the mainmast where it would be clearly seen in the morning. Then the crew took turns at the grindstone, sharpening their weapons, while one man kept an eye on the Spanish ships, and another watched for any movement on the shore.

Sparks flew from his cutlass as Tom put an edge on the blade. "Jack's a genius," he said to Dan who was waiting his turn. "This'll be a piece of cake."

"Yeah," said Dan, shaking his head. Tom's 'pieces of cake' usually took a lot of swallowing.

"And *you* get to fight as well," said Tom, almost

choking with excitement. "They're Spaniards, so you get to cut their throats with the rest of us. Great, eh?"

Dan shuddered at the thought. "Yeah, great," he mumbled as he took his turn at the grindstone and sharpened his knife to a wicked edge.

They crammed into the ship's launch, so tightly packed that they struggled to row, but Jack thought the Spaniards were less likely to spot a single vessel. The boat swept quietly across the night-black harbour, oars dipping in and out of the inky water. Dan crouched in the bow, peering into the darkness, praying they would reach their quarry without being seen or heard.

The huge bulk of the galleon loomed up and the bosun swung the tiller to take them wide around her bow. Dan held his breath as they passed the giant ship, but no challenge rang out. They set course for the sloop, and rowed on in silence. Even McKaig sat still and quiet, Thackeray's pudgy hand clamped tightly over his mouth.

They could make out the outline of the sloop now and the bosun took them around to the blind side where no-one from the galleon could see them climb aboard the ship. They heaved themselves up to the gunwale, checking for any sign of life before sliding silently over the rail.

McKaig's wooden leg clunked loudly on the deck. Calico Jack hissed at him not to move, then motioned fore and aft. Knife in hand, Mary Read crept towards the bow while Noah Harwood stole silently to the stern. Patrick Carty inched his way up the rigging in case they'd posted a lookout at the masthead. Jack led the rest of the pirates to wait like statues by the fo'c'sle door, with McKaig remaining at the rail.

Patrick Carty glided down from the mast shaking his head, but Mary Read and Noah Harwood both arrived back wiping bloody knives on the sleeves of their shirts.

Jack stood by the fo'c'sle entrance and motioned to the others. This would be where the crew were sleeping. He turned the knob and pushed. The door creaked and they froze, but no alarm went up. They crept through the doorway, each pirate stopping silently by a full hammock.

Dan hung back. When the last man had disappeared into the gloom of the fo'c'sle, he slid through the opening, praying that each hammock would already have a knife-wielding pirate lurking beside it. But the one nearest the door swung heavily with a snoring Spaniard in it and no one at his side. Trembling slightly, Dan inched forward and waited for the command. Sweat dripped into his eyes and the knife felt slippery in his hand. He could hear the rhythmic breathing of the sleeping sailor. The last breaths he would ever take. *He didn't think he could do this — but he had to. The man was an enemy and their own lives were at stake.*

"Now!" hissed Calico Jack and strong hands clamped over sleeping mouths. Knives rose and fell, hacking and slicing. Blood gushed unseen up walls and covered the living and dead alike.

"Alarma!" screamed a voice near the doorway. "Alarma!"

Mary Read leapt across the room, burying her knife in the man's throat as he made for the door. She kept stabbing

101

until the man lay still.

"How the hell did we miss him?" hissed Calico Jack.

Dan held onto the hammock, his unbloodied knife in his shaking hand. He hadn't been able to kill in cold blood. He said nothing.

The pirates crouched in the fo'c'sle, listening, sure that they must have been heard. No alarm was raised on the nearby galleon but sounds of activity came from the grand cabin. At a nod from Jack, Mary Read and Noah Harwood crept aft and disappeared into the night. Dan heard a door open followed by a muffled groan, then a dull thud as a heavy object was lowered to the deck.

Noah and Mary reappeared. "No more Spaniards back there," whispered the blood-stained woman. Dan shuddered.

"Shall we release the prisoners, if we find any," asked George Featherston.

"No," said Jack. "We leave things as they are until morning." He looked around him. "Does anyone else speak Spanish?"

"I do," mumbled John Howell.

"You take first watch then. Answer if we're challenged. Wake me in four hours and I'll take over. The rest of you, get some sleep."

Calico Jack made his way to the grand cabin, followed by Anne and Mary. Dan turned to the fo'c'sle. He could smell a mixture of blood, shit and piss, and decided against a comfortable hammock for the night. He settled down in the open and snatched what sleep he could on the hard deck.

A strong hand shook Dan awake as the first rays of sunlight speared across the harbour. Calico Jack stood over him, dressed in a blood-spattered Spanish lieutenant's uniform.

"Get below with the others. Out of sight," said Jack, fatigue and exhilaration mixed in his voice. "I'll stay on deck and call you when we need to get underway."

Dan took a deep breath then slid into the fo'c'sle. The stench of death assailed his nostrils, and he nearly gagged. Dead bodies swung eerily in blood-stained hammocks, arms and legs dangling carelessly over the sides. Others were piled on the floor, pirates having taken their beds as well as their lives. The rest of the crew crouched at the back of the room but Dan stayed near the doorway where a slight breeze carried some fresh air to his lungs.

A call came from the galleon and Calico Jack calmly waved a greeting then turned away. Dan could hear the bustle on the Spaniard's deck and his mind pictured the powder monkeys running to and fro bringing cartridges up for the guns, topmen swarming up the rigging to set the sails, and men toiling at the capstan to up anchor. He could hear the sound of grinding metal and knew that swords and boarding pikes were being sharpened on the Spanish ship.

Calico Jack moved to the fo'c'sle door. "We're anchored by the stern and the tides coming in so we're facing the wrong way — into the harbour. Thackeray! Take Dan, Needles and John Davis and drop the bow anchor. George! Stand ready by the stern anchor with an axe. Cut the cable when I tell you and that'll swing us about with the tide, bow facing the open sea."

As they heaved the anchor over the side, the cable

snaked around, rushing through the hawse hole. Thackeray poured a steady stream of seawater onto the wood to stop the friction sparking a fire.

Dan glanced at the galleon. The Spaniards didn't seem to have noticed anything strange on the sloop. They were too busy checking guns and setting canvas on the fore and mizzen masts. The Spanish ship began to nose gently into the harbour towards her prey.

Dan could clearly see *Santa Anna* bobbing in the gentle swell, the Jolly Roger billowing out in the freshening wind. The Spaniards spotted the flag and an angry shout went up. Men lined the rails, weapons glinting in the morning sun. The gun-ports snapped open and big, evil-looking muzzles appeared as the cannons were run out, ready for firing. All eyes on the Spanish ship were fixed on *Santa Anna*.

"Now!" called Jack and the bosun hacked through the stern cable with one huge blow from the axe. As the rope parted, the ship began to swing around, the bow held fast by the one remaining anchor.

Calico Jack signalled the topmen, and Patrick Carty, James Dobbin and Tom, hoisted the mainsail while Thackeray struggled with the smaller headsail.

"All other hands to the capstan," shouted Jack, and Dan hurried forward with the rest, straining to lift the anchor as the sails fluttered overhead and began to fill.

A thunderous roar hit them and Dan turned to see timbers flying from *Santa Anna* as round shot smashed into her side. Gun smoke soon obscured the view as it drifted across the harbour.

"Never mind the fireworks," screamed Calico Jack.

"Get that anchor up fast. Your lives depend on it."

Dan returned to the task, straining on the capstan bar, forcing his aching legs to push. Round and round they went, then the anchor pulled free and the work eased as they hoisted it up from the depths.

Another great blast echoed from the harbour and again Dan turned and stared at *Santa Anna*. Her mast had fallen and most of the quarterdeck had all but disappeared. Yet another broadside slammed into her and Dan felt a tight knot in his stomach, imagining they were still on board.

With the anchor up, the sloop began to make headway. Calico Jack put her on a starboard tack, tight into the wind.

"We're too slow," groaned McKaig, gaping at the destruction being rained on *Santa Anna*. "The wind's against us. We cannae get away fast enough."

George Featherston looked at the cut of the sails on the sloop, and then at the galleon. "We're as good as home," he said. "This sloop can sail closer to the wind than a square-rigger. This Northerly is a God-send. They'll never catch us if it keeps blowing. Once we're out of cannon range we're safe."

In the harbour, the Spanish galleon continued to pound the empty pirate ship, oblivious to the small sloop as it sailed silently away, Calico Jack smiling at the helm.

Calico Jack gathered the crew on deck. Having made sure that everyone was well armed, he ordered the prisoners released from the hold. They were all British naval ratings and not one would join the pirates.

"We'll set them ashore in Jamaica," said Jack.

Dan's heart leapt in his chest. *Jamaica! That was where he would find his father. He knew it.*

Scar scowled. "Why Jamaica? We marked men there."

"Not in this ship we're not," said Jack. "They don't know her. And Jamaica is where the rich pickings are. You all want to get rich, don't you?"

The pirates shouted their agreement and Scar stalked off to the fo'c'sle.

Jack turned to the prisoners. "As none of you have seen fit to join this noble crew, you will remain locked in the hold. You'll not be harmed. We'll put you ashore when we make landfall."

"You're making another mistake," said Mary Read. "They'll just add to the people in Jamaica who can name us as pirates. Drop them over the side. "

"I want them to live," said Jack, puffing out his chest. My name will be famous when these tars spread the word of how I plucked them out from under the nose of Spain. I can see the headlines now. *Bold Jack Rackham and the Spanish Galleon!* Now there's a tale!"

"You're a fool," snapped Mary. "A conceited fool!" She retreated to the cabin and slammed the door.

Calico Jack addressed the naval ratings. "Before you go below, I've got a little job for you."

He led them into the fo'c'sle and they re-emerged, ashen-faced, carrying the bodies of the slaughtered Spanish prize crew. After they'd tossed the corpses over the side, Jack ordered them back down into the hold.

"They'll have second thoughts now, if they were planning to take over the ship," said Jack.

He turned to Thomas Earl. "Needles, paint a new name on the stern. And don't let the prisoners know we've changed it. We'll call her the *Curlew*. She's slender and fast, and flies like a bird over the ocean. Oh, and sew up a new flag. A white skull above crossed swords as usual."

Dan thought about the Jolly Roger. "Why do you fly a pirate flag? Doesn't it give you away?"

"We only fly it when we know we'll catch our prey," said Jack. "It strikes the fear of God into them. Rather than risk our wrath if they run or fight, most merchantmen will heave-to and surrender their cargo at the mere sight of the Jolly Roger. Saves a lot of time and bloodshed. And I want them to know it's me." Jack preened himself. "It's not just that I like the notoriety. If they recognise my flag then they know I'll be merciful if they don't resist." His face hardened. "And that they'll die if they do."

Dan grimaced but nodded his understanding, then went to look for Tom. He found him at the main hatchway where he'd shut the British sailors in the hold. "Jamaica!" he said. "That's where I'll find my dad. I know it."

"What do you plan to do?" asked Tom.

"I'll ask Jack to put me ashore near Port Royal. Ask around for Daniel Leake."

"I'll come with you," said Tom. "You'd not get far without me, would you?"

Dan lowered his voice. "I'd love you to come Tom, but they won't let you go. You signed the *Articles*."

"Well I'll unsign them then. I'm coming with you."

"Thanks Tom."

"No problem, mate. We've got to stick together,

haven't we?"

Anne Bonny came over. "What are you two whispering about?"

"Dan's leaving us in Jamaica," said Tom quickly, not mentioning his own plans. "Going to look for his dad."

"Lickspittle Leake?" Anne pulled a face. "Well good luck with that."

Dan turned. "What do you mean by that?"

"Nothing," said Anne, moving away. "Nothing at all."

Dan watched her sway across the deck. "She's hiding something, Tom. She knows more about this 'Lickspittle Leake' than she's letting on."

CHAPTER 11

JAMAICA

The screaming pirates hurled themselves across the gap between the two ships, tearing into the merchant sailors, with cutlasses and knives. With several of their crew lying bleeding on the deck, the seamen threw down their weapons and surrendered. Another prize for Calico Jack. The sailors looked on helplessly as their cargo was plundered but, once they had everything of value safely stored in their own hold, the pirates let them sail away. They didn't have enough men to crew captured vessels.

The tranquil waters off Hispaniola had proved a rich hunting ground. The capture of two sloops and a schooner, had the pirates in high spirits, but every day was an agony for Dan who only wanted to get to Jamaica. He spent more and more time on his own, looking at the portrait in his silver locket.

When they put in to shore to replenish their supplies, Scar volunteered to go with the landing party.

"You're not thinking of jumping ship are you?" Dan asked him quietly. "Hispaniola's Spanish. They'd hang you wouldn't they?"

"Spanish welcome good sailor, and not care if slave," said Scar. "But this half of island, French. They treat slave worse than British do. No, Scar not run."

"Good," said Dan. "I'd hate to see you go." He looked closely at the big man. "I wouldn't have survived this long if I hadn't met you."

"You were boy then. Man now."

Dan still thought of himself as a boy, but sometimes felt like he'd lived a dozen lifetimes. He looked down at his arms where corded muscle reflected the hard toil of a life at sea, and he thought that maybe Scar was right. Perhaps he had grown up.

The shore party came back with water, a few goats and two captured Frenchmen. The reluctant captives were forced to join the crew to swell their numbers. With over half of their original ship's company dead on *Isla De Los Pinos*, they needed more men.

"Frogs," sneered McKaig, glowering at the Frenchmen. "We'd be better off signing on the goats and eating the Frogs."

"Aye, I like the taste of frogs' legs," said Thackeray.

The Frenchmen looked on wide-eyed.

"We'll not be eating anyone," Calico Jack assured them. "You're part of the crew now."

The next day the wind picked up and blew steadily from the east. With a following wind, the sloop danced over the waves and away from Hispaniola. Jack let Dan take the noon reading of the sun, and plot their position on the chart.

"If we bear north-west we should sight Jamaica

110

sometime this afternoon," said Jack. He turned to Dan who was grinning like an idiot at the mention of Jamaica. "I need a lookout up at the mast head."

Dan's face dropped and Jack looked at him thoughtfully. "Wake Tom and tell him to get up there."

Relief and guilt filled Dan in equal measure as he stood over Tom. He couldn't help smiling as his friend snored away like a lion, his face a picture of peace and contentment. "Landlubber!" he yelled at the top of his voice, and Tom sat up, his eyes half open and trying to focus. "Stop snoring your idle face off and get your backside up to the masthead."

"Aye Aye, Captain," croaked Tom and, swaying to his feet, he began to crawl up the rigging.

Halfway up he came to a sudden stop and glared down at Dan. "You're not the bloody captain!"

Dan grinned up at him. "Jack's orders," he called. "Lookout needed at the masthead. I'll take over at a quarter past never."

Tom flicked him a two-fingered salute but carried on up. He'd barely reached the top before he was bobbing up and down, waving his arms like a madman.

"Sail ho!" he called.

"Where away?" cried Calico Jack.

"Off the starboard beam!"

The captain moved to the rail and raised his spyglass to his eye. He called Dan to the quarterdeck and passed him the glass. "You've got young eyes. Can you see her colours?"

Dan squinted through the eyepiece. "It's a black flag."

"Pirate," grunted Jack. "Can you make out the device?"

Dan peered hard at the flag as it fluttered in the breeze. "It's a man with a flaming sword in his hand – standing on two skulls."

"*Royal Fortune*," gasped Calico Jack. "What the hell is she doing in these waters? I thought that lunatic was away plundering Newfoundland!"

"Who is it?" asked Dan.

"Black Bart, that's who!"

"Damn and blast!" George Featherston stared fixedly at the distant ship. "What are we going to do, Jack?"

"We're going to run, that's what we're going to do. Helmsman, hard a-larboard. Raise all sails."

Dan furrowed his brow. "He wouldn't attack a fellow pirate, would he?"

"Who knows? I'm not taking the chance," said Jack. "He's a madman."

"Aye," growled Thackeray, who'd made his way onto the quarterdeck. "And ye should see his *Articles of Agreement*. Proper cruel they are. No drinking; no women on board; bed-time at eight o'clock; church parades on Sunday mornings. The man's a monster!"

"And he'd throw the Irish overboard before he did anything else," said Jack.

Dan blanched. "Why the Irish?"

"His second in command, an Irishman called Kennedy, sailed off in one of Black Bart's ships. He's been hunting him ever since but, in the meantime, any Irishman will do. He kills them on sight. You'd be well advised to stay clear of him."

Dan gulped and nodded his agreement.

With all sails set, the sloop out-distanced the pursuing ship and finally left it over the horizon. As soon as he dared, Calico Jack lowered the spinnaker and turned north.

They sighted land the next day.

"It's Jamaica," said the bosun and Dan felt his heart leap. He climbed up the rigging for a better view of the island, praying that nothing would go wrong this time. He'd miss his shipmates, but he wasn't a pirate. Their casual attitude to violence still shocked him. *He wasn't like that. He wasn't a pirate.*

Tom interrupted his thoughts, clambering up and swaying on a foot rope next to him. "Didn't expect to find you up here!" he said, staring towards the distant island. "I thought you hated heights?"

"It's not so bad when the sea's calm," said Dan, though he felt himself going dizzy as he looked down. He'd been alright until Tom had mentioned it.

"I love it up here," sighed Tom, turning to take in the horizon in every direction. "I love this life!"

"Well I don't," said Dan. "I want to find my dad and settle down again — on dry land." He looked pointedly at Tom. "And you've got a family in Bristol. You'll be wanting to get back to them, won't you?"

"Maybe for a while. But I'll go to sea again. This is what I want to do. I was born for this."

"Piracy?" asked Dan sharply.

"Er... I meant a life at sea. I might even join up again."

"The Royal Navy? You've got to be kidding. It's brutal. You're at the mercy of a bunch of sadists!"

"I kind of liked it," said Tom sheepishly. "Apart from the noise of a twenty-five-gun broadside. And I guess I'd get used to that after a while."

Dan shook himself. He was shocked that he found it easier to understand someone becoming a pirate than volunteering for the navy.

By late afternoon they'd reached the coast of Jamaica. Dan gazed at the long golden beaches with their green, tree-lined backdrop.

"I'm dropping the prisoners off in Montego Bay where they'll not be able to cause us any mischief. Then we'll make for Port Royal on the other side of the island." Calico Jack eased the helm to larboard. "We can re-provision there and have a few days' rest. I think we've earned it."

Dan found Anne Bonny leaning on the starboard rail. She was hatless and her long, auburn hair flowed down over her slim shoulders. "Hi Dan," she said brightly. "To what do I owe this rare pleasure?"

"Um, hello." *Why did he always sound like the village idiot when he talked to her?* "Lickspittle Leake," he muttered. "You said he lived in Port Royal, didn't you?"

"Nearby," she replied. "He has a plantation nearby."

"I'm going to find him when I get ashore," said Dan quickly, unable to keep the excitement from his voice. "I think he could be my dad."

She looked at him with sad eyes. "You might be disappointed, Dan."

"I don't think so. I've thought about it and I'm pretty sure he must be my dad."

Anne Bonny held his eyes for a moment. "You still

114

might be disappointed."

Dan shook his head. *Sometimes she made no sense at all.* He left her and climbed back up to the quarterdeck where he told Calico Jack his plans.

"You're free to do as you please, Dan," said Jack, taking off his tricorn hat and running his fingers through his long, straw-coloured hair. "But I'll be sorry to see you go." He held out his hand and Dan shook it. "We'll be in dock for a week or so. If things don't work out for you then you know where to find us. You're always welcome to sign on."

"Thanks Jack," said Dan, surprised at the lump that had grown in his throat at the thought of leaving the pirate band. He decided to try his luck. "Is it okay if Tom comes with me?"

"Of course," said Calico Jack.

Dan nearly hugged him in surprise and delight.

"As long as he's back by the end of the week," added the captain. "If he breaks his oath and deserts then if any of us see him again we'll cut his throat."

Dan's face fell, his chest tightening. He swallowed hard. "I'll make sure he's back," he said in a small voice.

The sun was setting as they sailed into Port Royal. Jack gave everyone shore leave, as they'd have taken it anyway. "Come on, Dan," shouted Tom as he scampered down the gangplank. "I'll race you to the nearest tavern."

"I'm not going to an alehouse," said Dan. "I'm looking for my dad. I need to find Daniel Leake."

"At this time of night? Where do you think you're

going to find him? Everywhere's shut apart from the bars."

His shoulders slumped and Tom put a hand on his arm. "Cheer up mate. Come to the tavern. I bet we'll find someone who knows him."

Dan allowed himself to be led to a grimy, dimly-lit building on the water front. "I think we can find a nicer place than this," he muttered, looking warily at a sign that read, The Skull and Crossbones.

"It'll be fine," said Tom, disappearing through the door.

Dan sighed and followed him in.

A wall of noise hit them as they entered. Everyone seemed to be singing, shouting, or laughing. Gaudily-painted women swayed through the crowd, carrying drink trays, deftly avoiding groping hands and playfully slapping leering faces. Others perched on customers' knees, swilling rum straight from the bottle and screeching with laughter.

The men were a bloodthirsty-looking gang of cutthroats, but Dan realised with a start that Tom and he looked little different from the rest. Tom seemed perfectly at home and squeezed onto the end of a bench at a busy table, waving Dan to sit opposite him. A man with a scarred, weather-beaten face shifted up good-naturedly and made room for Dan as Tom called for rum.

"Where have you two sprung from then?" asked the scarred man.

"We're from the *Curlew*," said Tom, snatching a bottle of rum from the tray of a passing waitress and holding out a Spanish piece-of-eight. She pocketed it with a speed that amused Dan and handed over a second bottle.

"Anything else you want sonny, just give Nell a call." She treated Tom to a gap-toothed smile and zigzagged away through the boisterous crowd.

"I think you overpaid her," chided Dan.

"Got to keep 'em sweet haven't you?" laughed Tom, passing a bottle to Dan. "She'll look after us now."

"Never heard of her," said the man.

Tom raised an eyebrow. "I beg your pardon?"

"*Curlew*! Never heard of her."

"Oh!" said Tom. "We've just renamed her. Used to be called something else."

"That figures. Most ships around here used to be called something else." The man laughed then turned his attention back to his bottle of rum.

"I'm looking for someone," said Dan. "Daniel Leake!"

The man froze mid-drink then slowly lowered the bottle to the table. "Who did you say?" His voice was a low growl.

"Dan," said Tom. "I think—"

"Daniel Leake," repeated Dan. "Have you heard of him?"

The man turned and studied Dan's face for the first time. His eyes narrowed. "You're called Dan. Your surname wouldn't be Leake, would it?" There was no trace of friendliness in the growled question or on the hard face.

"Dan," warned Tom, "I think we'd better—"

"Yes. I'm Dan Leake."

"Daniel Leake!" The man rose to his feet. The rest of the table had gone quiet and other heads were turning in their direction.

"You're Lickspittle Leake's son?" roared the man. You could hear a pin drop in the hushed bar.

"I... I... don't know," stammered Dan, looking around him. "I think I might be."

"No misbegotten son of that turncoat is welcome here!" the man shouted. A rumble of agreement echoed around the bar. Men were rising to their feet.

"But why–"

"Come on Dan." Tom tried to pull him from the table but the man grabbed Dan by the arm, his face contorted. Tom hit him hard between the eyes and the man fell backwards over the bench.

"Come on!" Tom pulled Dan towards the exit. A bottle smashed over the doorway as the boys fled from the bar.

A few drunken men staggered into the street after them but soon gave up the chase. They slowed down to a walk and moved along the waterfront.

"Your dad doesn't seem very popular around here, mate," said Tom, stopping to catch his breath.

"I'm not surprised," said Dan defensively. "That place was a nest of pirates. They're not going to like a Royal Navy officer, are they?"

"Officer?" Tom arched an eyebrow.

"You don't know my dad!" snapped Dan. "He'll be an officer by now."

"Okay, okay! He's an officer. But I think it might be better if you don't mention him again tonight. We'll ask around in the morning."

"You could be right," agreed Dan, glancing back over his shoulder. "I'll wait until morning."

They reached another inn. A large sign announced it as The Three Horseshoes. "Come on," said Tom. "I'm buying."

Dan hesitated. "Tom, I don't really…"

But Tom was already pushing through the door.

The small bar was busy but not as raucous as the previous one. They took the last two places at the end of a long bench table and again Tom called for rum. They sat in silence for a while, Dan trying to make sense of what had just happened, when the door burst open and Anne Bonny and Mary Read staggered in, dressed as men but giggling like twelve year old girls. They spotted the boys and swayed over.

"Hello lads," slurred Mary. "Can we join you?"

"There are no seats left," scowled Tom.

"Oh, I don't know about that," said Mary, planting herself on his lap. "This one's pretty comfy."

Tom's scowl deepened.

"Your friend's not much of a gentleman," said Anne. "How about you, Dan?"

He got up and offered her his place.

"How come Mary gets a nice comfy seat and I have to sit on a hard, wooden bench?" teased Anne, but she sat down anyway.

Dan glanced about for a spare stool but Anne put an arm around his waist and pulled him onto her knee. He reddened as faces turned towards them.

"You boys are a bit friendly aren't you?" smiled a one-eyed sailor beside them. "You're not at sea now you know. There are plenty of wenches about."

Mary Read unbuttoned her shirt and flashed her chest at the man. His one eye nearly popped from his head. "Oh, I see," he said and took a long swallow of his rum. He turned his eye on Dan. "I suppose you're a girl as well?"

Tom's drink sprayed from his mouth as he half choked on his laughter. Dan tried to struggle to his feet but Anne held him on her lap, giggling worse than ever.

Mary Read put an arm around Tom. "Are you going to buy us a drink, lover?"

"No!"

"Don't be like that," she said, making a grab for Tom's bottle. He pushed it out of her reach.

Anne Bonny called for two rum punches and bounced Dan on her knee.

"Will you stop that," he hissed, trying to squirm off her lap. But she held him tight, surprising him with the strength in her slim arms.

"The Three Horseshoes," sighed Mary, a gentle tone in her voice that was new to Dan. "I once owned a tavern in Holland called, The Three Horseshoes."

Dan gave up trying to escape Anne's clutches. He was only succeeding in amusing everyone. "How did you come to own a tavern in Holland, Mary?"

Tom groaned. "Don't encourage her."

"I was in the army, disguised as a man," said Mary.

"And it's a great disguise," interrupted Tom. "Especially the moustache!"

She slapped the top of his head playfully, then her eyes turned soft again. "I met a Flemish soldier and Mother Nature got the better of me. I let him find out I was a woman and we ended up wed. That shocked the army — two of its soldiers getting married. They gave us a discharge." She smiled at the thought. "We bought a tavern with the loot we'd taken on the campaign and settled down to married life."

"I can't see you as the settled type," said Dan.

"I was very happy — until the fever took him." A tear formed in her eye and rolled slowly down one cheek. "He was a lovely man. Tom reminds me of him." She stroked Tom's hair, and he pulled his head away.

"What was his name?" asked Dan.

"Something Van Something," said Mary. "I could never pronounce it."

"Very romantic," muttered Tom.

Mary planted a kiss on his cheek. Tom shuddered.

"I couldn't run the place on my own so I took a ship to America, hoping to start a new life. But the ship was taken by pirates. You know the rest. You were there. You were the pirates."

"We're not pirates," snapped Dan.

Tom quickly began studying his fingernails.

The rum punches arrived and Anne Bonny snatched up the bottle that Tom had placed out of Mary's reach. "Just livening up my punch," she said as she upended it into her drink.

"That must be the liveliest punch in history," groaned Tom, weighing the half empty bottle in his hand.

"Have mine," said Dan, pushing his bottle across the table. "I'm not a great one for the rum."

"Oh, but you've got to have a drink," said Anne.

121

"We're celebrating."

"Celebrating what?"

"Who cares? Try mine."

Dan took a sip of the rum punch and a slow smile spread over his face. He'd never tasted anything like it. Flavours he'd never known before mixed and blended on his tongue, and the rum added a pleasant kick to it.

"Nice, huh?"

Dan admitted it was.

"Have it," said Anne and ordered another.

Several rum punches later, Dan was feeling talkative. He tapped the one-eyed man on the arm. "I'm Dan," he slurred.

"Is that short for Daniella?" grinned the man.

"Daniel. Daniel Leake!"

"Shut up," hissed Tom but the man was already staring fixedly at Dan.

"Daniel Leake," rumbled the man. "I know a 'Daniel Leake'."

"That's my dad," said Dan.

"Daniel Leake's your father?"

"I think so. Do you know where I can find him?"

"Aye, I do."

Dan rapidly began to sober up. "You do?"

"You'll not find him this time of night, not round here anyway, but if you take the Yallahs Road in the morning you'll find his place. Plantation about two miles out of town on your left. Big white house on the hill. You can't miss it."

A smile slowly widening on his face, Dan turned to

Tom. "I've found him!" He started laughing. "I've found him! I've finally found him!"

Tom raised his bottle. "Let's have a drink to celebrate!"

"No!" said Dan. "I need to be sober for tomorrow. I'm going back to the ship."

"No need," smiled Anne Bonny. "They've got rooms at this place. We can stay here."

Dan struggled to his feet and quickly stepped out of reach. "I'm going back to the ship."

"Don't go yet," begged Tom. "Have another drink."

"*You'll* stay and keep us company, won't you lover?" Mary Read put her arm around Tom.

"I've got to make sure Dan's alright," blurted Tom, jumping to his feet and dumping Mary on the bench. "Here. Have my rum." He shoved the bottle into her hand and started after Dan.

"I've never seen you give up your rum before," grinned Dan.

"Well, anything for a mate."

"Yeah, right!" said Dan, the smile broadening on his face.

Tomorrow he was going to find his dad.

CHAPTER 12

LICKSPITTLE LEAKE

Dan rose with the sun and shook his friend from his sleep.

"Leave me alone, Mary," Tom groaned. "I'm tired."

"Wake up Tom! It's me!"

"What? Oh! Sorry! I was having a nightmare."

"Yeah! I guessed. Get up. We're going to find Daniel Leake."

Tom rolled out of his hammock, fully clothed and stinking of rum.

"Well that saves a bit of time I suppose," said Dan, wrinkling his nose and pulling a face. "Let's go!"

"Not until I've had some breakfast," yawned Tom, rubbing his stomach.

Dan twitched and fidgeted as Tom took his time over a bowl of broth and a scrap of dry bread. "Can't you hurry up?"

"Nearly done." Tom slowly ran the crust around the empty bowl before wiping his mouth on his sleeve. He burped loudly and patted his belly. "I'm ready!"

Tom stumbled along the gangplank after Dan. "Will

you slow down?"

"Sorry," said Dan. "I can't help it. This might be my dad we're going to see."

"And it might not," warned Tom. "You shouldn't get your hopes up."

"I know, but I've got a good feeling about this. My dad's close. I can sense it."

The dockside had already come to life, men bustling around, loading and unloading the ships lining the quay. They passed a row of chained men shuffling to the auction blocks, their pale European faces downcast, many calling out in Irish until whips snapped them into silence. Slavers drove a ragged mass of sullen, coal-black Africans down the gangplank of another ship to join the general melee. Tom stared open-mouthed but Dan pressed on, too excited to notice. He set off up the Yallahs road with Tom trailing behind him.

The large whitewashed house gleamed in the morning sunshine and Dan stopped and stared, his heart beating like a hammer in his chest. Dark figures toiled in the surrounding fields, cutting sugar cane.

"Are we going in or not?" asked Tom, beating dust from his trousers.

"In a minute," said Dan. "Just give me a minute."

After a short while they made their way up a long, sweeping path to the house, and climbed the steps to a wide veranda where Dan hesitated a moment before knocking on the big, brass-handled door. It creaked open and a stooped, white-haired black man stood there.

"Is Mister Leake at home?" asked Dan.

"Depends on whom's callin'," drawled the man.

"Is he in or not?" snapped Tom.

The old man regarded him coldly.

"Who is it, Ruben?" boomed a voice from inside. A tall, thick-set man with dark hair greying at the temples, came to the door.

"They didn't say, Massa."

Dan gaped at the man, his eyes wide and his whole body trembling. He tried to speak but no words came.

The man looked them up and down, taking in their tattered clothes and weather-beaten faces. "Set the dogs on them," he said, turning away.

"I'm Dan! Dan Leake!"

The man froze, then slowly came back to the door.

"Dan?" He stared intently into his face, the silence dragging on. "No, you can't be! Dan's just a kid."

"It's been nine years," said Dan, fumbling in his pocket. "Kids grow up."

He pulled out the locket and passed it to the man who hesitated then opened it and found himself staring at his own portrait.

"My God Dan, it is you!" He gaped at the locket for a moment, shaking his head, then slowly straightened up. He held out his arms and Dan flew into them

"Dad, I knew I'd find you. I knew it!"

Daniel Leake prized Dan off and held him at arm's length, studying his face. "You've got your mother's look about you, so you have. What are you doing here? How did you find me?"

"It's a long story," said Dan, gazing into his father's

face, drinking in the older but still familiar features.

"I'm forgetting my manners, so I am. Who's your friend? Tom Bailey? Pleased to make your acquaintance young man. Come in. Come in, the pair of you."

The large entrance hall faced a wide, ornate staircase leading up to a balcony that overlooked the hallway on three sides. A crystal chandelier hung from the ceiling high above their heads.

Tom spun slowly around, mouth open and eyes wide. "Your old man's done alright for himself," he whispered.

Dan turned to his father. "I've got so much to tell you," he gushed. "And so many things to ask. I don't know where to start."

"Later!" said Daniel Leake. "I've some matters to attend to. But you'll join me for lunch, won't you?"

"Yes, but–"

"No buts. I have to go." He smiled an apology. "Ruben! See that these two young gentlemen have a warm bath and a change of clothes. Have Lily attend to it. Oh, and throw out those rags they're wearing." With that he strolled out the door.

Elation and frustration flowed through Dan in equal measures. His father had just seen him for the first time in nine years. He thought he'd burst with all the words and emotions fighting to get out, but now he'd have to keep them bottled up for hours. *How could he just walk out?*

Tom, brow furrowed, stared at the tub full of steaming water. "What do we need a bath for? It's not Christmas, is it?"

"You stand there stinking then. I'm having one." Dan climbed gingerly in, then relaxed as the warm water flowed soothingly around his limbs. He stretched out and gave a long, contented sigh. "You don't know what you're missing, Tom."

A pretty mulatto maid walked in with another pitcher of hot water. Dan jumped up, then quickly covered himself with his hands as she glided over and emptied the jug into the bath.

"Do you want me to wash you?" she asked.

"N-No! I can manage!" stammered Dan.

The maid hesitated for a moment, then nodded and left.

"'N-No! I can manage!'" mimicked Tom. "What's the matter with you?"

"I… Well… She caught me by surprise, didn't she," said Dan, reddening. He quickly changed the subject. "What did you think of my dad?"

"I don't know. He didn't hang around long enough to tell. But he seemed happy enough to see you."

"I'm *more* than happy to see *him*. I can't believe he walked out."

"You can't just call on someone after nine years and expect them to drop everything. He looks like an important man. He'll have things to do. He's probably gone to cancel his appointments so he can be with you this afternoon."

Dan sighed. "I guess you're right." He leant back in the bath and tried to relax again. "It's just that, after nine years, when he saw me… I don't know. I expected more."

"You're talking daft. Look at this place. You've fallen

on your feet and no mistake. Don't look for problems that aren't there." Tom glanced at the door that the maid had disappeared through. "And hurry up! I think I'll take that bath after all."

Dan felt stiff and awkward in a starched white shirt and knee-length black britches pulled down over silk stockings. Silver buckles sparkled on his black, square-toed shoes. His only consolation was that Tom seemed even more uncomfortable. He grinned as he regarded his friend. In bright orange pantaloons and purple shoes and shirt, he looked like a peacock — but he wasn't strutting. He was glowering at the mirror.

"They've burnt my clothes! How can I go back to the ship looking like this? They'll slit my throat for the buckles on my shoes, if they don't die laughing first."

The door opened. "Dinner is served," announced Ruben, resplendent in a black, knee-length coat. He led them down to the dining room.

A long, highly-polished oak table faced them with Daniel Leake seated at its head, two giant Irish Wolfhounds at his feet. He waved the boys to their places either side of the table. "Did you enjoy your bath?" he asked Dan with a smirk. "I hope Lily got you nice and clean."

"I washed myself," said Dan.

His father frowned. "I gave orders for her to wash you. I'll have her flogged for this."

"You whip your servants?" gasped Tom.

"She's a slave! And she does what she's told, or else."

The boys sat in shocked silence, Tom wriggling uncomfortably in his chair.

Dan found his tongue. He didn't want anyone beaten on his account. "She offered," he said. "But I refused."

"I can get you someone else if she doesn't please you?"

"I'm quite capable of washing myself," said Dan, and his father sighed.

Ruben placed three steaming bowls in front of them, before retreating from the room. Dan stirred the soup idly with his spoon, thinking of Scar. There was a sour taste in his mouth. "Are all your workers slaves?"

"All except Ruben. I freed him years ago, but he won't leave. Says he's nowhere else to go. He runs the house for us."

"Us?"

"Me," said Daniel Leake quickly. "Oh, and there's Liam O'Connor, my supervisor."

"He's not a slave?" asked Dan.

"No. An orphanage sent him over from Ireland ten years ago as an indentured servant."

"So he can come and go as he pleases?"

"Well, no. He has another four years to serve."

"And he's been working for you for ten years?"

"No. I bought him three years ago."

"You bought him? And you could sell him if you wanted to?"

"Yes, but–"

"He's a slave, Dad. You're keeping a fellow Irishman as a slave!"

Lickspittle was unfazed. "Most of my slaves were Irish

when I first started out."

Dan's eyes flashed. "But *you're* Irish. How could you do that?"

"I'm running a business here Dan, and Irishmen are a lot cheaper than Africans. But you get less work out of them. They're more rebellious and they have an annoying tendency to die from sunstroke. Nothing but trouble. I replaced them with Negroes as soon as I could afford it."

He saw the look on Dan's face. "You don't approve of Irish slavery?"

"I don't approve of *any* slavery!" snapped Dan.

"You can't run a plantation without slaves. You'll come to realise that when you've been out here a bit longer."

Dan sat brooding, his untouched soup in front of him.

His father broke the silence. "How did you get to Jamaica? How did you find me?"

'I wish I hadn't,' thought Dan, then instantly felt bad for thinking it. *This was his father. Maybe he wasn't perfect, but he was sure he meant well. He'd talk to him about freeing his slaves. He'd already made a start with Ruben, hadn't he?* "I joined the navy. I thought they'd know where you were. But then I fell overboard in a storm. Tom and another friend jumped in to help me. We were picked up by… by a ship, and they brought us to Jamaica. One of the crew said she knew you."

Daniel Leake went very still. "She?"

"Her name's Anne Bonny."

The older man slowly lowered his spoon and placed it in the bowl in front of him. "You sailed with Anne Bonny?" His eyes narrowed as Dan nodded. "What sort of ship was it? What was the cargo?"

Dan felt himself colouring. "I... I think they may have been... they may have been pirates."

An oppressive silence dragged slowly by.

"You didn't sign on, did you?"

"No, I didn't. They tried to make me but I wouldn't."

"Good lad. That took courage, so it did."

The praise swept over Dan like a warm balm despite his earlier anger.

His father picked up his spoon and hovered over his soup. "Anne Bonny. What did she tell you about me?"

"Nothing really. Just that you were here and that you once sailed with her." Dan stopped then whispered, half to himself, "You sailed with Anne Bonny." He looked closely at his father who stared into his untouched soup. "How come you were sailing with Anne Bonny if she's a pirate?"

Daniel Leake looked up but didn't meet Dan's eyes. "I was a... a business associate of her husband. It was before the pair of them turned pirate. It was just a merchant ship."

As Dan stared at him, his father continued to avoid his eyes. *He was lying.* Dan felt the heat rush to his face, his fists clenching and unclenching, nine years of hurt flowing through him. "And why aren't you in the navy anymore?" His voice rose. "And why didn't you come home to Mum and me?"

His father sank into his chair. "I was discharged from the navy years ago. I was in Jamaica and didn't have the fare to get home, but I did have a few business propositions. My plan was to make some money then send for you and your mother."

"Well you made your *money*, didn't you?" Dan let the real question hang in the air unspoken.

"Life got in the way, Dan. Things out of my control. I did mean to send for you." Daniel Leake looked up. "How is your mother anyway?"

"Dead!" snapped Dan. "Dead this last year."

"I'm sorry to hear that."

"Are you?"

His father lowered his eyes. "I really am. Who's been looking after you?"

"I've looked after myself. I'm not a kid anymore."

"No, I can see that, Dan. I can see that."

They sat in silence for a while, only Tom eating. "Delicious," he said, pushing the empty bowl away from him and burping loudly. "What's for the main course?"

The other two remained silent. Eventually the older man spoke up. "What are your plans, Dan? You'll be staying the night of course?"

Dan moved his hands under the table. He didn't want them to see his tightly clenched fists. He took a couple of breaths to steady himself. "Stay the night?"

"You're more than welcome. And your friend as well, despite his manners."

"Stay the night!" Dan's whole body shook, his stomach a pit of writhing vipers. "You've been gone nine years. I've spent months searching for you. I've fought a battle; been lost at sea; survived pirates and cannibals, and had a ship shot from under me by the Spaniards to get here. And I can stay the night?"

133

Daniel Leake seemed to physically shrink. He rocked back in his chair. "You've got to understand. Nine years is a long time. Things are complicated."

"Well, I don't understand. I'm your son! You're all the family I have."

"It would be awkward if you stayed longer, Dan."

"Awkward? Look at the size of this place. How awkward could it be?"

The older man stared at the floor and said nothing.

"Come on, Tom. We'll not stay where we're not welcome!" Dan jumped to his feet, sending his chair clattering to the floor behind him.

The wolfhounds growled.

Tom hesitated, his eyes not on the dogs but on Ruben who hovered by the door, plates of steaming food in his hands.

Daniel Leake stood up. "Dan, I'm sorry. Please stay. At least for the night. It's just… this has all come as a shock. We'll work something out."

"Listen to him," said Tom. "You've come all this way. You can't just walk out now! At least sleep on it."

"Please Dan. Sit down," pleaded his father. "I need to think. I do care for you. Of course I do. But, like I said, things are complicated. I need time to think."

"Come on Dan, sit down," urged Tom.

Dan struggled with his emotions but eventually picked up his chair and returned to the table. Ruben hesitated then approached and placed plates of boiled goat, sweet potatoes and yams in front of each of them, removing the soup bowls. Tom wolfed his down as Dan and his father sat in brooding silence.

Ruben woke them early for breakfast, not that Dan had slept much. The conflicting thoughts battling in his head had refused to let him rest. That and Tom's contented snoring. They dressed then made their way down to the dining room.

Daniel Leake sat at the table, reading a dog-eared paper. "Ah, boys! Sit down. Sit down!" They took their seats, Tom greeting him cordially, Dan in silence.

Tom soon demolished a breakfast of ham and eggs. Dan pushed his food around the plate, Daniel Leake regarding him thoughtfully.

"I'm sorry I can't let you stay, Dan. Sure it doesn't mean we can't see each other. Let me know where you're living. If money's a problem, I can put you up in Port Royal. I own some property there, so I do."

Dan's head hung on his shoulders. "But why can't I stay? Why can't I stay here with you?"

"It's awkward Dan. I'll explain some other time." He glanced at the large pendulum clock by the wall. "But right now, you have to leave. I have… guests arriving in half an hour."

Dan rose slowly to his feet, his legs struggling to support the heaviness in his soul. He turned to the door which suddenly burst open, and two young boys ran in with Ruben in close pursuit.

"I'm sorry, Massa," croaked the old man, worry creasing his face. "I tried to stop them."

The children threw themselves on Daniel Leake.

"Daddy, Daddy," they cried, both jabbering away at the same time.

Dan froze.

A tall, regal-looking woman in a long, flowing, sky-blue dress swept in. She stopped when she saw Dan and Tom.

"I'm sorry, Daniel," she said, her voice high and plummy. "I didn't know we had company."

"That's alright, Dear. They were just leaving, weren't you, gentlemen?"

Dan remained where he was, rocking on his heels, bile rising in his throat. A small sob escaped his lips, and he bit it back.

Tom stepped forward, his face red but his eyes cold flint. He took hold of Dan by the arm. "Let's go, Dan," he said loudly. "We'll not stay a second longer under this bedswerver's roof."

As Tom pulled him to the door, Dan heard the woman. "Who are those dreadful people, Daniel?"

"No-one, Darling. They're no-one."

CHAPTER 13

BETRAYAL

Back on the *Curlew*, Tom struggled for words of comfort as he watched his friend slumped in a corner of the fo'c'sle, hugging his knees to his chest.

"Dan, I'm sorry…"

"Please Tom. Just go. I want to be alone."

Tom hesitated, biting his lip. He reached out and gently squeezed Dan's shoulder before moving to the door. "I'll be around if you want me, mate. Just give me a shout."

Dan said nothing and Tom shuffled out on deck, his blond eyebrows knitted together in consternation.

"How is he?" Anne Bonny took one look at Tom's face. "Not good, huh?"

"No, not good. His father's a toss pot."

"I could have told him that."

"Then why didn't you?" snapped Tom.

"He wouldn't have listened to me. He had to find out for himself."

Tom's voice rose as he struggled to control his temper. "How could you let him walk into that house, knowing what you did?"

"I didn't know he'd added bigamy to his list of crimes," said Anne, leaning away from Tom's anger.

"Well what *do* you know about him then?" Tom knew it wasn't Anne he was angry with, but he couldn't keep the edge from his voice.

She hesitated then shrugged. "I first met Dan's father…"

"Don't call him that," spat Tom. "He's no father to Dan!"

Anne sighed. "I first met him when I was sailing with Charles Vane. Leake was a small-time pirate back then."

Tom's head jerked up. "He was a pirate?"

"Not a very successful one but yes, he was a pirate."

Tom slowly shook his head. "He looks successful to me."

Anne Bonny's face darkened. "That's not how he made his money." Her voice was a low growl. "Lickspittle Leake and my darling husband, they took the King's Pardon in the Bahamas when the governor offered an amnesty to any pirate who would give up the life. And the ones who refused? Those two sold their names and whereabouts to the authorities." She spat on the deck. "They bought their plantations with the lives of their old shipmates."

Tom let out his breath in a slow whistle.

"Yes," said Anne. "They're a proper pair of charmers. Daniel Leake came to Jamaica and carried on selling out his old pirate friends to the new governor here. He's that hated, there are places in Jamaica where it's dangerous to even mention his name."

"Yeah, I noticed," muttered Tom. He looked up to the heavens for inspiration but found none. After a few moments he turned back to Anne Bonny. "How am I meant to tell all that to Dan?"

"And you expected *me* to tell him when he still hero-worshipped his father? At least now he has some idea of what he's really like."

The days passed slowly as they provisioned the ship and Calico Jack tried unsuccessfully to recruit more men. Dan spurned any attempts to get him talking. He shunned company while he brooded, caught up in his own thoughts. Only Scar could get close. The big man seemed happy to sit with him without the need to talk - a towering, silent, comforting presence.

As the week drew to an end, Jack called Dan to his cabin. "We sail with the morning tide. Are you staying with us or going ashore?"

"I'm staying with you," said Dan. He had nowhere else to go.

Calico Jack pushed a document across the desk. "Sign!"

Dan looked down. It was the *Articles of Agreement.*

He picked up a quill and leant over the paper. His hand shook as he held it above the inkwell. After a few moments he straightened up, dropping the unused quill back on the desk. "No. I'll not sign. I'm not a pirate!"

"For the love of…!" Calico Jack threw his hat on the floor then took a deep breath. He leant back and slowly ran his hands through his long hair. "It may have escaped your attention, but this is a pirate ship. We don't provide a passenger service. We saved you from the sea but now you're safe in port. If you want to sign on, you're more than welcome. If not, then you go ashore."

"Please Jack! You're the only friends I have."

"Then join us. Sign!"

Dan screwed his eyes shut and rubbed his temples. "Please, give me some time to get my head together. I need to think."

"You've had months to think about it, Dan."

"But things have changed. I thought I had family here. I thought wrong."

Jack sighed. "I'll give you one month, Dan. At the end of the month you either sign or you leave the ship."

Dan nodded and let out the breath he'd been holding. He went on deck and climbed out onto the bowsprit where he could be alone to try to make some sense of the world he now found himself in.

In Spanish Town, a cigar in one hand and a glass of wine in the other, Daniel Leake relaxed in the governor's office. Sir Nicholas Lawes regarded him keenly over the rim of his glasses. "You didn't get the name of the ship?"

"No."

"But, Anne Bonny, you say? Here in Jamaica? In Port Royal?"

"That's right. And where you find Anne Bonny you'll find Calico Jack, so you will." Daniel Leake's eyes narrowed, searching the governor's face for any sign of deception. "I want the price on both their heads – and the rest of the crew as well."

"And you'll get it. Your help has been invaluable to me, Mr Leake. Since Woodes Rogers became Governor of the Bahamas and clamped down on that pirates' nest in Nassau, they've come swarming over to Jamaica. If they think they'll find a safe haven here they've got another thing coming."

The governor's voice rose and his colour heightened as he warmed to his theme. "I'm going to wipe them out – every man jack of them." He paused and took a long swig of his wine. " 'The golden age of piracy', some are calling it. Well that age is over. They've had their day and now I'm going to send them screaming into the night!"

Repaired and resupplied, the ship was ready to sail on the morning tide. As it was to be their last night ashore, Tom tried to persuade Dan to go into town. He refused, still shunning the company of others despite his desperate loneliness. Tom gave up and went ashore with Thackeray and McKaig, even though they now called him, 'Peacock', and constantly teased him about his new clothes.

Drunken shouts woke Dan as the crew staggered back on board in the early hours. He drifted off to sleep again and when he arose he found the pirates sprawled across the deck in drunken stupors. Calico Jack and the bosun kicked them awake and held a roll call. Thackeray and McKaig were missing.

Jack swore. "Does anyone know where they are?" His voice was a mixture of anger and concern.

Tom stirred and held his throbbing head in his hands. "Erm... They were still in The Three Horseshoes when I left last night."

"Then get yourself back over there and see if you can find them. And hurry!"

As Tom staggered down the gangplank Calico Jack shouted to the crew. "We sail with the tide whether they're on board or not. Prepare the ship."

The men stumbled to their stations, faces green and hands shaking as they set about their work.

Tom returned. There had been no sign of the two missing pirates.

"They wouldn't desert us," mused Jack. "The old fools will be snoring in a gutter somewhere with their pockets picked. But, we'll not be waiting for them."

A flash of colour caught Dan's eye, and he looked up. Red-coated soldiers swarmed at the end of the quay. Dozens more flowed down into a row of small boats at the water's edge. Heart pounding, he shouted the alarm.

"Hell's teeth!" yelled Calico Jack, looking frantically around him. "George, have we enough water beneath us to get under way?"

"Aye, but the tide's against us. It's still coming in."

"But we could make it out of the harbour?"

"Not as fast as they can row," said the bosun, pointing at the rowing boats pushing off from the quayside.

"We're dead men then," said Jack, as yet more redcoats hurried along the wharf towards them.

Suddenly the quay emptied as the troops boarded a brig four ships down from the *Curlew*. The rowing boats surrounded a sloop in the centre of the harbour, soldiers swarming up the sides like and army of red ants.

"If it's us they're after, they don't know which ship we're on," yelled Calico Jack. "Cast off! Set the sails."

The bosun bellowed the captain's commands and the crew ran to carry them out, the lethargy of moments ago forgotten.

"All hands to the sweeps!" called Jack, and the crew man-handled the long, heavy oars into the water, Scar and Thomas Bourn leaping back on board after casting off the mooring ropes.

As the topmen secured the sails, the rest of the pirates heaved and grunted at the sweeps, slowly edging the sloop away from the quay. Calico Jack kept his eyes on the soldiers. They were still busy rounding up the crews on the other ships and had not yet noticed that the *Curlew* was under way.

As they inched closer to the harbour entrance, the wind became stronger, and they began to make way against the tide. A sudden shout went up from behind and Dan turned to see men pointing in their direction, and soldiers pouring over the sides of the other sloop and back into the fast rowing boats.

"Pull," yelled Calico Jack. "Pull for your lives!"

Sweat pouring from them, the pirates redoubled their efforts, gasping for breath under the hot morning sun. Dan joined Tom who gave him a half-smile as they toiled at the heavy sweep. The sloop picked up speed but the row boats were skimming over the water, closing the gap with every pull of their light oars. They reached the harbour entrance with the soldiers right under their stern.

"Bring in the sweeps! Prepare to repel boarders!"

shouted Jack.

The pirates grabbed weapons and ran to the gunwales.

As the *Curlew* eased out into the Caribbean, the sea breeze filled her sails and the ship jumped forward, the rowing boats losing ground as they reached the choppy waters outside the harbour.

"Down!" yelled Calico Jack, and they hit the deck as the soldiers fired a frustrated volley harmlessly over the heads of their fast-retreating prey.

The pirates cheered as Scar fired the stern-chaser, capsizing one of the pursuing boats. The soldiers, weighed down with heavy equipment, floundered in the dancing water, other boats giving up the chase to rescue their drowning comrades.

Minutes later the *Curlew* was out of range and racing along the coast. Tom laughed as the tension dissolved. He clapped Dan on the back.

"You've got to love this life, haven't you mate? You've got to love it."

CHAPTER 14

CAPTURED

For the next few weeks the *Curlew* cruised the south coast of Jamaica, probing into small bays and inlets, searching out prey. Dan's mood swung back and forth. One day he'd decide that he could live this life after all, but then they'd board a small fishing boat and steal her nets and tackle. Another day he'd be struck by the kindness of his rough companions as they tried to lift his spirits, but then they'd take an unarmed ship and hold down her captain, pricking him with knives until he revealed where he'd hidden a handful of coins.

"It can't be helped," said Jack when Dan chided him for picking on poor, working boats. "I want to go for rich merchant ships, but they're armed and ready. Our company's too small to take them, and we haven't enough men to crew them if we did. So we have to play at the low game until we can increase our numbers. And that means taking fishing boats and small coastal ships. At least we'll eat." Jack swatted at some flies with his hat. "Believe me, I'd rather be out at sea with a fresh breeze, Spanish galleons and no damned flies, but we need more men. I'm heading for Negril. There'll be a few lads there looking for an honest living. Not everyone's cowed by the governor, like those lily-livered swabs in Port Royal." Jack regarded Dan ruefully. "Talking of recruits, I need your answer. Are you staying or going?"

Dan swallowed hard. "I'll give you my answer tomorrow, Jack. I promise."

"See that you do!"

"Sail ho!" came a shout from above. Calico Jack rammed his hat onto his head and hurried out on deck with Dan close behind him.

A large schooner had pulled out of a bay straight in front of them. When they saw the Jolly Roger, they tried to make a run for it but the pirates had the weather gage and soon overhauled them. Calico Jack hailed them and offered them life or death. They chose life and surrendered without a fight.

The pirates boarded the schooner and herded the crew together. The master of the ship gave his name as Thomas Spenlow and Calico Jack took him up to the quarterdeck to question him about his cargo.

George Featherston, as he often did, addressed the captured crew. "Your captain," he asked, "is he a fair man or a tyrant?"

Like many others, the bosun had turned to piracy due to harsh treatment doled out by a sadistic captain in the merchant marine. They held the power of life or death aboard a ship. Now, as a pirate, *he* held that power, and he used it on captured captains.

The sailors whispered amongst themselves then one

stepped forward. "He's a hard man but a fair one," he said. The others nodded in agreement.

"His crew hold him to be a fair man," the bosun shouted up to the quarterdeck.

"Congratulations, Mister Spenlow," said Jack amiably. "You'll not be swimming with the sharks. You may take your officers ashore in the jollyboat. I'll be keeping the ship and your crew."

"They'll not join you," spat Thomas Spenlow. "They're all honest hands."

"We'll find out how honest they are," said Jack, cleaning dirt from under his fingernails with a sharp knife.

He shouted down to the bosun. "Put the captain and his officers in a boat and send them on their way."

Thomas Spenlow, along with his first mate, quartermaster and bosun, sculled away towards shore, hurling curses back at the pirates. Jack ignored them and put the question to the captured sailors. Their captain had been right. Not one man would join the pirates despite all Calico Jack's threats and promises.

"We can't take the schooner without its crew," whispered the bosun. "We've barely enough hands to man this sloop as it is."

Jack punched his fist into his hand. "How much more money do we have to throw away for lack of men?" He stamped up and down the quarterdeck, cursing and swearing. "I've a good mind to press the lot of them."

The bosun moved closer, keeping his voice low. "It's too dangerous, Jack. They outnumber us. We could be overpowered if they've the stomach for it."

"Alright!" snapped Calico Jack. "Strip the schooner of anything of value then send them on their way."

"Aye Aye, Captain." The bosun left Jack fuming on the quarterdeck.

Calico Jack's mood had not improved the following day as they sailed on around the west coast. He paced the deck, his face like the thunderclouds that gathered briefly above them before blowing out to the Atlantic. Dan kept well forward, out of view. His time had come to an end and, in this mood, he had no doubt that Jack would put him ashore if he remembered. He had to make up his mind. He didn't want to be a pirate but the thought of being alone and friendless in a foreign land terrified him.

Mary Read came to stand beside him. "Penny for your thoughts."

Dan looked at her closely. "You enjoy this life, don't you?"

"Aye, I do!"

"But how can you? I mean, if you're not killed in a fight, then one day you'll be captured and hanged."

"I wouldn't have it any other way," said Mary. "If it wasn't for the fear of hanging, every coward would turn pirate and the seas would be so infested with them that we'd starve. No merchant would venture out to sea and piracy wouldn't be worth following. It's only the fear of hanging that keeps rogues honest, so I say hang us. Hang every pirate caught and let fear keep the oceans free from the plague of 'honest' men."

She left Dan deep in thought.

Tom found him skulking near the bows, trying to avoid

an encounter with Calico Jack. "Have you made your mind up yet mate?" he asked. "They're not a bad bunch on board, admit it."

"They're pirates, Tom."

Dan fiddled with the cuffs of his shirt. They were already beginning to fray, the fine cloth too soft for a life at sea. He wondered if he was like the cloth. The expensive shirt made him think of his father.

"I didn't give my dad a chance to explain, did I? I was thinking about going to see him again. See what he's got to say for himself."

"A bunch of lies, that's what he'll have to say. Dan, you've got to accept that your dad's a bas–"

"Don't talk about my father! You don't know him!"

"You don't know him either." Tom played his trump card. "Did you know he was a pirate?"

"Yes, I guessed. Why do you think we fell out at his place?"

"Oh!" Tom scratched his head. "I didn't know why you fell out. Not until his wife and kids came in."

Dan's face dropped.

"I'm sorry Dan, but he abandoned you and married again when he was still wed to your mum. What am I meant to think of him?"

"I've got to hear it from *him*, Tom. I have to know why. He was a great dad when I was little."

"Well he's not now!" Tom looked carefully at Dan. "Do you know how he got the money to pay for that plantation?"

"Piracy. Yes, I know."

"It wasn't piracy. He sold out his old shipmates to the governor. Saw them all hanged. That's why they hate him in Port Royal."

"You're lying!"

"I'm not, Dan."

"You're lying! You've turned pirate and you're lying to get me to stay. Well, I won't!"

"But Dan…"

Dan stormed away, leaving Tom alone in the bows.

They reached Negril Point and sailed around the spit, into Bry Harbour Bay. A small pettiagua bobbed at anchor close to the shore. *Curlew's* bow-chaser belched flame as the bosun put a shot across her bow.

"What did you do that for?" yelled Calico Jack as the fishermen scuttled into the ship's boat and rowed frantically for shore.

"I've saved us a fight," said the bosun. "They've abandoned ship. We can walk on board and take her."

"We need a crew, not another ship," barked Jack. "How are we going to get them to join us now?"

The sailors reached dry land and clambered out of their boat.

"Take us as near to shore as you dare," said Jack. "I'm going to hail them."

The bosun took the helm and brought them close to the beach with 'Old Dad' Fenwick swinging the lead and calling out the depth marked on the attached line.

Calico Jack shouted to the men who gathered warily on the beach, armed with cutlasses and a few old muskets.

"My apologies if the shot alarmed you gentlemen. We only meant to salute you, not scare you."

"You've got our ship. What more do you want?" called a small, swarthy man.

"We don't want your ship," declared Jack. "Are you Englishmen?"

"Aye, we're English."

"Then come on board and share a bowl of punch with your countrymen."

"What do you want from us?"

"Just some fellowship over a few bowls of punch, that's all."

The small man made no move.

Calico Jack looked around at his crew then back to the captain of the fishing boat. "We're only a small company including two women and two lads. There are ten of you. You can bring your weapons on board. We've more to fear from you than you have from us."

The men on the beach held a quick debate. Stranded on a deserted stretch of shore, they had few options. The strangers had made no attempt to board their boat, and they could see no reason why they'd want to harm them when they could take their vessel without a fight.

"Alright," shouted the Captain. "We'll come aboard but we'll be keeping our weapons with us, and if you try anything we'll be using them."

"Come aboard then," bellowed Jack, jovially. "Come aboard!"

The jollyboat nudged alongside the *Curlew* and the sailors climbed warily aboard, muskets or cutlasses in hand. The captain introduced himself as John Eaton. Jack clapped him on the back and called for rum. Hours later, as they opened a second barrel, weapons had been laid aside and the merchant crew were talking and laughing with the pirates. Dan chatted briefly with Benjamin Palmer, a timid thirteen-year old from the merchantman, but he was in no mood for a party and soon moved away to be alone, his thoughts on his own uncertain future.

Calico Jack studied John Eaton carefully. "We mean you no harm but I'll not lie to you." He paused, making up his mind. "We're pirates."

"I'd guessed." The captain of the pettiagua smiled at Calico Jack's puzzled expression then pointed upwards. "That was a bit of a giveaway."

Jack looked up at the black flag and laughed. "I'd forgotten to take that down." He took a swig from his mug and carried on. "The pickings round here are rich. We've seized several ships, but we don't have enough men to crew them or to take on the big merchantmen where the real money is. We're after decent sailors to join us."

"And that's why you've asked us aboard?" The captain's hand strayed to the hilt of his sword.

"It is," admitted Jack. "But I'm only after volunteers. Our company is too small to have men on board against their will, so you've nothing to fear from us. But why scrimp a living in that little scuttlebutt of yours when you could join us and live like kings?"

"Or die like dogs!" said the captain.

"We all have to die. It's how we live that matters, and it's a good life. You'd still be captain of your own crew but sail under my command. We'll soon get you a bigger ship and more men. You'd get a captain's share of any booty and your men would get equal shares with my crew. What do you say?"

John Eaton squirmed uncomfortably, rubbing his throat with his hand. "I don't fancy a noose around my neck. I'll not be joining you, but ask my men if you wish. I'll not stand in their way."

"I'll do that," said Jack, climbing to his feet and calling for silence. "Lads! If you haven't already guessed what we are, I can tell you. We're pirates!"

Jack's crew gave a cheer and the merchant sailors laughed nervously, some of them pulling discarded muskets closer.

"We mean you no harm," put in Jack quickly. "We're looking for volunteers to join us."

The sailors whispered and murmured to each other.

"Listen to me for a moment," cried Jack, and launched into a monologue about the joys and benefits of a pirate's life. Dan felt himself being caught up in Jack's enthusiasm. The way he put it, it didn't seem such a bad thing.

The men from the pettiagua argued among themselves for a while, then a tall, thin man called Thomas Quick spoke up. "What say you, Captain?"

"I'll not be joining," said John Eaton. "But let each man decide according to his own conscience."

The muttered debate started again then Thomas Quick rose to his feet, running a bony hand through his thinning hair. "We've been drinking," he said. "Some of us can't

153

think straight. We'll give you our answer when we've sobered up."

Calico Jack nodded. "Well you'll not be sobering up for a while," he said. "Bosun! Break open another barrel."

The men shouted their approval.

Dan moved further away from the party. He had his own decision to make today. He climbed up to the quarterdeck and leant against the taffrail, gazing thoughtfully out to sea. A flash of white caught his eye, and he turned his head. Another flash. A sail? Then there it was. A heavily armed sloop-of-war ghosting around the spit and into the bay.

"Jack!" he yelled. "A ship! There's a ship in the bay!"

The pirates stumbled to the rail and stared, open-mouthed, at the sloop. A white ensign flew from her stern. They were staring at their own death.

"Cut and run!" screamed Calico Jack and men hacked desperately at the anchor rope with hatchets as the drunken topmen struggled into the rigging.

A sudden scream followed by a sickening thump sent the hairs on the back of Dan's neck on end. Patrick Carty had drunkenly missed his footing and plunged to the deck. Anne Bonny and Mary Read dragged him, squirming in pain and clutching his right leg, into the fo'c'sle.

The tipsy topmen managed to hoist the sails but the winds were light in the bay and the momentum was all with the warship swooping in from the Caribbean.

"Man the sweeps!"

Men jumped to the heavy oars. The fishermen, caught up in the moment, heaved on the sweeps alongside the pirates. The ship slowly picked up speed but the sloop-of-war steadily ran them down then 'went about' to bring her guns to bear as she turned broadside on to the *Curlew*.

A deafening roar rent the air and round shot ripped through the ship, bringing down the mast and taking off Thomas Quick's arm at the shoulder. John Davis lay squealing on the deck, the fallen yardarm across his shattered legs.

The warship sailed on past the now motionless sloop then turned back to bring her starboard broadside to bear.

"Man the guns!" shouted Jack.

"You man them!" Richard Corner ran for the safety of the fo'c'sle.

Panic took hold and the rest of the men bolted after him.

"Stand and fight! Stand and fight!" Anne Bonny and Mary Read beat at the men with the flats of their cutlasses but there was no stopping them.

Calico Jack clutched the rail, gaping at the fast-approaching sloop-of-war. The gun-ports opened and muzzles of death appeared as they ran out the big guns. He turned and staggered after his fleeing crew.

Mary Read, screaming in rage, tried to physically drag the cowering men from the fo'c'sle, but they pushed her out and barricaded the door. Apart from John Davis, still trapped under the yardarm, only Dan, Tom and Scar remained on deck with Anne Bonny and Mary Read. The warship, seeing what had happened, veered towards them, ready to board.

Mary Read hammered her fists against the fo'c'sle door. "Come up and fight, ye cowards. We'll hang if we're taken. If there's a man among ye, ye'll come up and fight!"

The door remained firmly barred.

Cursing and swearing, Mary Read snatched the pistols from her belt and fired them through the door. Two screams answered the report of her guns, and her contorted face softened briefly as she smiled in satisfaction. "Chicken-livered milksops!" she yelled then threw down the empty pistols, drawing her cutlass and turning to face the sloop-of-war as it pulled alongside. Anne Bonny joined her, screaming defiance at the sailors lining the rail of the warship.

Tom pulled out his cutlass and started forward but Scar snatched if from his hand.

"Ship taken," growled Scar as Tom whipped around. "Raise weapon and hang. Do nothing - might live. Tom not pirate by choice. Pulled from sea."

"So were you," said Tom, knocking the cutlass from the big man's hand and kicking it overboard.

"But Scar not want to live!" snarled the giant. "Scar die before go back as slave!"

As the warship's crew came screaming over the side, Scar let out a roar and charged across the deck, knocking three men overboard with his bare fists before disappearing under a horde of kicking, punching bodies. Anne Bonny and Mary Read fought ferociously but eventually had the bloody cutlasses knocked from their hands before being beaten to their knees.

"Take them alive," shouted the officer. "Save them for the gallows." He banged his fist on the fo'c'sle door. "This is Captain Barnet. Your ship is taken. Unbar this door and come out."

"Why should we?" slurred a drunken voice from within. "You'll only hang us."

"I'll burn the ship down around your ears if you don't come out. Hang or roast, it's all the same to me."

Moments later bolts scraped behind the door then it creaked open and Calico Jack shuffled out followed by the rest of the crew. The sailors disarmed them and shackled them together.

"We're not with them," protested John Eaton. "That's our boat over there. We just came on board for some punch. We didn't know they were pirates."

"Save it for the judge," snapped Captain Barnet. "I saw you and your men at the sweeps, trying to escape us."

"But we… I…"

"Lock them all in the hold, Bosun."

The sailors forced them deep into the bowels of the ship then battened down the hatches, leaving them in the dank, brooding darkness.

CHAPTER 15

THE TRIAL

In Port Royal, the pirates sweated and swore in their black, humid, windowless cell. The stench of excrement assailed Dan's nostrils, and he fought to choke back the vomit that gathered in his throat. They'd been locked in this airless hole for over three weeks and the sores around his ankles, where the leg-irons bit in, had started to fester.

The room stilled as keys rattled in the door. It swung open and the gaoler stood there, his bald head glistening with sweat and his fat, heavy jowls quivering.

"Good news," he grinned. "Your trial's tomorrow and you'll hang the day after that. My brother's the hangman so it'll all be nice and friendly. A family affair. Now enjoy your meal."

He moved aside and two guards carried in a large pot of lukewarm goat stew. The gaoler hawked loudly then spat in the pot. "Got to have your greens," he smirked.

The pirates shuffled over in their shackles and the guards ladled stew into their out-held tin mugs. A new tub of water was left in the room and the old, long-empty one taken out as the prisoners thirstily slurped down their ration.

"Why are *we* still here?" moaned John Eaton. "We've done nothing wrong. Why are *we* still locked up?"

The crew of the fishing boat grumbled their agreement.

"Don't worry," said Calico Jack. "We'll speak up for you. *We're* as good as dead but there's no point in you lot swinging alongside us."

"As good as dead?" snapped Anne Bonny. "Speak for yourself. I've no intention of hanging just because you men were too cowardly to fight."

Calico Jack flinched as if he'd been struck. "We were drunk," he complained. "We were in no fit state to fight. And it was hopeless anyway."

"Nothing's ever hopeless," ranted Anne, her small hands clenched into fists. "Not while you've breath in your body and the will to live."

Jack regained his composure. "And exactly how do you intend to escape the hangman?" A sad smile played across his face. He'd resigned himself to his fate and had urged the others to do the same. "There's only one place we're going, so make your peace with God and confess your sins. Lord knows we've committed enough of them. Who amongst us doesn't deserve to hang?"

"I've no intention of hanging, whether I deserve to or not," said Anne. "I'm going to plead my belly!"

Calico Jack's head jerked up. "You're with child?"

Mary Read brightened. "I'm going to plead my belly as well."

"As if," whispered Tom. "The man's not been born,

brave enough to board *that* ship!"

Thomas Earl poked John Fenwick's large stomach. "Why don't *you* plead your belly, Old Dad?"

"Why don't you go boil your head?" barked the cooper.

Jack took Anne Bonny by the arm. "You're with child?"

"I'd claim it even if I wasn't, but yes, I'm with child."

"And is it… is it…?"

Anne glared at him for a second then her green eyes softened a little. "Yes, Jack, it's yours."

Calico Jack let out a long sigh. "Then live, Anne. Live and tell our son his father wasn't a bad man, despite what he'll hear from others."

"I'll tell our *daughter*. But for her sake, not yours."

Scar settled down in a corner with Dan and Tom. "Dan should live," he rumbled. "Dan not sign *Articles*. Fall overboard then pirates pick up." He peered through the gloom at Tom. "Tom must swear pirates force him sign *Articles,* then Tom might live too."

"I can't do that. I'll be under oath. I'll not perjure myself."

"You sign *Articles* because not want throat cut," snapped Scar. "Remember?"

"Erm… Yes. That's true." Tom frowned as he thought. "Alright. I'll do it."

"And so will you, won't you Scar?" put in Dan. "You were forced to sign as well. We'll speak up for you."

"Scar plead guilty!"

Dan gaped at the big man. "What? Why?"

Scar leant against the stone wall of the cell. "If plead

'not guilty', they check. Find out runaway slave. Quick death at end of rope better."

They lapsed into an unhappy silence until sleep finally came and rescued them from their thoughts.

"Rise and shine!" shouted the fat gaoler, rattling a tin mug across the iron bars of the cell door. "You're off to the courthouse for a fair trial before they hang you all in the morning."

The prisoners climbed wearily to their shackled feet and shuffled out past the gaoler and his club-wielding guards. Red-coated soldiers loaded them into two large carts, and they set off for Spanish Town.

The courthouse was a large, whitewashed building directly across the square from the Governor's Residence. The guards forced twenty-four men and women into a dock meant for no more than twelve. John Davis, his broken legs still unset, lay in a stretcher at the side. The governor himself sat opposite them with two Royal Navy Post Captains as his fellow judges. There was no jury.

Calico Jack regarded the stern, unforgiving faces of the judges. "I'm surprised they haven't got their black caps on already," he muttered.

"Black caps?" asked Dan.

"They put on black caps if the sentence is to be death," whispered Jack.

Sir Nicholas Lawes started the proceedings. "You are accused of piracy on the high seas. If convicted, the sentence will be death." He paused and glowered at the dock for a moment, letting his words sink in. "How do you plead?"

The dock erupted in a cacophony of noise.

"Silence," yelled the governor, banging his gavel on the bench before him. "I will hear from you one at a time. Sit down and then stand when I call your name."

"There's no room to sit," complained Old Dad the Cooper. The others muttered their agreement.

The governor studied the gavel, turning it over in his hand. "Sit them down, Mister Gaoler, if you please."

Batons rose and fell until the prisoners squatted on their knees, crushed together, bleeding and cowed.

"Thank you," said the governor quietly, then turned his attention back to the dock. "John Eaton. How do you plead?"

The captain of the pettiagua struggled to his feet, blood streaming from a scalp wound. "I really must protest," he blustered.

"Protest noted," said the governor, waving it away. "All I need to hear from you now is your plea. Guilty or Not Guilty?"

"Not Guilty!" John Eaton, red in the face, shook with righteous indignation. "My men and I, we're not part of this pirate crew. We just went on board to drink some punch with them."

Sir Nicholas curled his lip into a sneer. "If you drink with scum you will be treated as scum." He turned to the court. "Call Captain Barnet to the stand."

The officer spoke in a strong, assured voice. "When I gave chase to the pirate vessel, my sloop clearly flying the White Ensign so they'd know we were a King's ship, I saw

John Eaton and his men pulling on the sweeps with the other pirates – trying to escape us."

"But I… We…!" stammered the prisoner before being waved to silence.

"And," went on the Captain Barnet, "when we boarded the vessel, John Eaton and his men barricaded themselves in the fo'c'sle with the rest of the pirates. They were not prisoners. They were armed, but they made no effort to help the King's men. They aided and abetted the pirates in trying to evade justice."

"But we…we…!"

"Silence!" shouted Sir Nicholas. He regarded John Eaton coldly. "It is clear to me that you were aboard that ship willingly and that you aided them in their attempt to escape justice. I therefore hold that you were all part of the *Curlew's* crew and, if they are found guilty of piracy, then you will share their fate."

John Eaton's mouth worked like a goldfish but no words came out. He blinked rapidly then, head bowed, sank heavily to his knees.

The governor's cold, grey eyes swept along the dock. "Before I proceed, is there anyone else who believes they're a special case?"

Scar nudged him but Dan stayed where he was. "What's the point," he muttered. "If he'll not listen to men who were only on board for a few hours, what chance do we have when we were there for months?"

"Has Dan seen man hang?" whispered Scar darkly.

Dan swallowed hard. "Yes!"

"Then speak!"

But it was the carpenter's mate, who stood up.

"Your name?" asked Sir Nicholas, irritation etched in his voice.

"John Howell of the *Dolphin*. And I'm not guilty. They took me from my ship and pressed me into their service against my will."

Dan and Tom listened intently, their own lives tied to how the carpenter's case would be considered

"You were on the *Dolphin* you say," mused the governor as he leafed through a sheaf of papers on the bench. "Ah yes," he said, producing two documents. "Are you familiar with the names, Stuart Henderson and Brian Alcock?"

"Yes," said John Howell. "They were shipmates of mine on the *Dolphin*."

"I have their affidavits here." The governor made a show of studying the documents. "It appears that you were the only member of the crew to turn pirate. You and a 'Mark Read', but he hasn't been apprehended."

"Yes but..!"

"They say that you volunteered?"

"I had to. They'd have killed me if I hadn't."

"The rest of the crew refused to turn pirate, but they were not harmed."

John Howell's face reddened, sweat sheening on his forehead. "They killed our captain. I thought they'd kill me too if I said no."

Sir Nicholas nodded to the court clerk. "Make a note please. John Howell testifies that the prisoners murdered the captain of the *Dolphin*."

Calico Jack groaned.

"So, they killed your captain but, when they asked for volunteers, only you stepped forward. How do you explain that? Were you the only coward on board? Are you a coward John Howell?"

The carpenter straightened up. "No, sir!"

"Make a note please, Mister Clerk. John Howell admits that he is not a coward and therefore it was not fear of death that made him join the pirates." The governor turned back to the carpenter. "Sit down thank you, Mister Howell."

"But I... I..."

Sir Nicholas nodded, and the gaoler beat the carpenter to his knees.

"Anyone else?" The governor glowered at the prisoners, defying them to stand up.

Anne Bonny and Mary Read rose up, to the obvious annoyance of Sir Nicholas Lawes.

"So, what nonsense have *you* to say for yourselves?"

"I'm with child." Anne Bonny's voice was clear and calm. "I plead my belly."

"Me too," said Mary Read.

The governor sighed and placed his gavel slowly on the bench in front of him. "And who are the lucky fathers?"

Both women pointed to Calico Jack who shrugged and smiled as Sir Nicholas fixed him with a disapproving glare.

He turned on Anne Bonny, the distaste ripe on his tongue. "I understand that you're a married woman! I should have you flogged for adultery before you hang."

"I plead my belly," repeated Anne, her calm gaze not faltering.

"I heard, blast you," barked the governor. "You'll both be examined later. Meanwhile, I intend to finish this trial. Sit down!"

The two Frenchmen who had been pressed in Hispaniola were not put on trial. They were called as witnesses for the prosecution. They accused Calico Jack and his crew of piracy but backed up John Eaton's story that his men had only gone aboard the *Curlew* for a few hours to drink some punch. Sir Nicholas waved them contemptuously from the witness box before they could finish their evidence.

Dorothy Thomas, the owner of the fishing boat they had plundered earlier in the year, condemned them all as pirates, picking out Anne Bonny and Mary Read as the most bloodthirsty of the crew, stating that they had both demanded her death.

"Then pray tell me how you come to be alive?" asked Sir Nicholas.

"Calico Jack!"

The clerk spoke up. "She's referring to John Rackham, Your Honour."

"I know who she's referring to," snapped Sir Nicholas.

"Calico Jack," repeated the woman. "He stood up for me. He's a proper gentleman he is."

"He wouldn't know a gentleman if one bit him on the arse!" The trial was beginning to fray Sir Nicholas' nerves.

Mary Read glared at Calico Jack. "I warned you. Your weakness has condemned us all. No witnesses would have meant no trial."

"Until we meet our maker," said Jack. "That's when

we'll really be judged. And I worry for your soul, Mary. I surely do."

Captain Thomas Spenlow took the stand and testified that Calico Jack and his crew had seized his ship off Negril Point the previous month. Again Mary Read glared at Jack but this time said nothing.

Sir Nicholas straightened and addressed the court. "Is there anyone who wishes to speak for the accused? No? Very well then." He raised his gavel.

Someone at the back of the court cleared his throat loudly, and the governor hesitated. Dan turned to see a well-dressed man step out into the aisle and stride purposefully towards the judge's bench. He gasped as the man came closer. It was his father.

"Sir Nicholas," said Daniel Leake as he stopped in front of him. "I beg a word in private."

"This is a court of law, Mister Leake. If you have anything to say then take the witness stand. Evidence must be given under oath."

Dan's father remained where he was. "I will take the stand if I must, but I beg a word in private first. It's a matter of some delicacy."

The governor wavered.

"My actions have had some bearing on this case," said Daniel Leake. "Surely it's not too much to ask for ten minutes of your time?"

Tom looked at Dan who shrugged.

"Very well," said Sir Nicholas. "I could do with something to eat anyway." He brought his gavel down. "The court will adjourn for lunch."

"I thought we'd adjourned for lunch?" complained Tom. They were back in a cramped prison cell and there was no sign of any food.

"His lunch, not ours," said Dan.

Tom held Dan's eyes. "Your dad, he's going to save you, isn't he?"

"I want nothing to do with him."

"Don't talk daft, lad." Calico Jack had overheard their conversation. "If you get a chance to live, take it. If you can't stand the man then walk away once you're out — but get out first. You've got your whole life ahead of you."

"Listen to Jack," said Tom. "Who knows, you might be able to talk your dad into getting Scar and me out as well."

Dan nodded slowly. "I'll try but I doubt he wants me out. I'm an embarrassment to him, aren't I? I'd get in the way of his cosy new life and family." He lowered his head, not wanting his friends to see the tears welling in his eyes.

Sir Nicholas Lawes paced up and down in the judge's chambers, his half-eaten meal of bread and cheese abandoned on his desk. "Your son you say?"

"Yes, Dan Leake is my son. Sure it's awkward because I didn't tell my wife I'd been married before and had a child back in the old country. I don't want her to find out. Not like this."

The governor stopped pacing and stared down his nose at Dan's father. "I trust you divorced your old wife before you took a new one?"

"She's dead, Sir Nicholas. She died a long time ago," he lied. "I thought Dan was dead as well, but he'd been in an orphanage. He ran away to sea to find me. Joined the Royal Navy and fought bravely for his country, from what I've heard."

"And then deserted." The governor's voice was still frosty.

"He fell overboard and his friends Tom Bailey and... I didn't catch his name, jumped in to save him. They had the misfortune to be picked up by a pirate ship and they were forced to sign the *Articles*. But Dan refused. He's a brave lad, so he is."

"It's an unlikely tale."

"You can check with the Admiralty easily enough to see if they lost three men overboard from...the *Dover*, I think he said. And you've got the *Articles of Agreement* from the *Curlew*. You'll not be after finding Dan's name there."

Sir Nicholas sat down behind his desk and rubbed his chin. "It will take time to verify their stories. They'll have to stay in gaol until then."

"You can release them into my custody. I'll make sure they turn up for trial when you call them. You have my word on it."

"What about your wife? You said it would be awkward."

"I'll put them up in my town house. Say they're business associates. But don't worry, I'll make sure that they're guarded."

"Very well," said the governor. "But you'd better make good on your promise."

He finished his meal and washed it down with a large glass of red wine. "Right then, back to the trial." He gave a satisfied smile. "I've got some death sentences to hand out."

The men and women packed into the courthouse, stood as the governor entered and took his seat between his fellow judges. As he sat down, a wave of expectation rippled around the room. A smattering of friends of the accused sat stony-faced, assuming the worst, but most people were there for the entertainment and the room buzzed with suppressed excitement.

Sir Nicholas cleared his throat. "Dan Leake. You will stand."

Tom patted him on the shoulder and Dan rose uncertainly to his feet.

The governor frowned. "Someone has come forward to speak for you. I understand that you were serving in the Royal Navy as a volunteer. A rare thing these days, and something to be commended. You fell overboard and were unfortunate enough to be picked up by this pirate scum."

He paused, his cold eyes ranging over the ragged men and women in the dock before turning back to Dan.

"I note that you did not sign the *Pirate Articles*, although I'm sure you were under intense pressure to do so. I also have the word of Captain Barnet that you were not armed when the *Curlew* was taken, that you did not resist and that you did not barricade yourself in the fo'c'sle with the pirates. I am therefore inclined to believe you innocent of all charges of piracy and, if my learned colleagues agree, I am minded to release you forthwith."

The two other judges nodded their assent and Sir

Nicholas instructed the gaoler to strike the shackles from Dan's ankles.

"You may leave the dock."

Dan hesitated. "It wasn't just me who fell overboard, sir. My friends–"

"Tom Bailey!" called the governor, ignoring Dan.

Tom jumped up. Sir Nicholas noted that, like Dan Leake, he wore dirty but finely-cut clothes, unlike the rest of the riff-raff. That made his mind up.

"I believe that you also served in His Majesty's Ship *Dover*, and that you jumped overboard to save your friend. Whilst this might be admirable, I note that you did sign the *Articles* aboard the pirate vessel and therefore you do have a case to answer. However, while this court is awaiting confirmation of your story from the Admiralty, I am willing to release you into the custody of Mister Daniel Leake, if you give me your word that you will not try to escape before your trial is reconvened."

"You have my word, sir," said Tom and, at a nod from the governor, the gaoler removed his shackles as well.

Sir Nicholas Lawes again scanned the dock. "I understand there was a third man picked up from the *Dover*, but I don't have his name."

"Algernon Lynch," blurted out Tom.

"Shut up!" hissed Scar from the corner of his mouth.

"Algernon Lynch," called the governor. "On your feet."

Scar remained where he was.

"Algernon Lynch. Stand up!"

The huge man slowly rose to his feet, his head bowed. The governor regarded him coldly. "A Negro," he spat.

He turned to where Daniel Leake now sat on the front benches. "Are you willing to vouch for this... this man? To take him into your custody?"

Daniel Leake looked askance at the giant black man. "No, sir. I am not."

Dan felt the bile rising in his throat as his father turned away.

The governor turned his attention back to Scar. "And how did you come to be serving in the Royal Navy?"

Scar said nothing.

"Answer me or I'll have you beaten!"

The gaoler moved closer, his baton in his pudgy hand. Scar still remained silent. Sir Nicholas nodded to the turnkey.

"He's mute!" shouted Dan, as the man raised his club.

"Is he indeed," said the governor, waving the gaoler away. "Then perhaps *you* can tell me how he came to be on board the *Dover*?" He studied Scar's downturned face. "And how he came by that scar on his cheek?"

Dan swallowed hard, trying to think quickly. "He was already aboard when I signed on. He's a gun captain. He got that scar fighting the King's enemies."

Sir Nicholas continued to stare at Scar. "Or else he's a runaway slave, and he cut the brand from his own face. I've known it done before."

Scar visibly slumped. Dan had never seen him look so small. All the life seemed to have drained from him, leaving an empty husk.

"I will need to look deeper into your case, Lynch. In the meantime, as no one is willing to vouch for you, you will continue to be held in gaol. Take him away."

Two of the guards led a listless, unprotesting Scar, from the court.

As the rest of the prisoners prayed and fidgeted in the dock, the governor conferred with his fellow judges, then motioned to the clerk.

"The court will rise," called the official.

The audience jumped to their feet, the excitement tangible in the crowded courtroom. The prisoners rose slowly, heads bowed, awaiting their fate.

The judges reached down then straightened up, each placing a black cap on his head. A roar of approval erupted from the crowd, and a low moan from the dock.

"Silence in court!" yelled the governor, banging down his gavel.

When the noise had subsided he addressed the prisoners in the dock. "You have been found guilty of piracy on the high seas. The sentence is death. Tomorrow you will be taken to Gallows Point and hanged by the neck until you be dead. May God have mercy on your souls."

Another cheer went up.

"But I plead my belly," cried Anne Bonny over the uproar. "You can't hang an unborn baby!"

Sir Nicholas glared down his long nose at her then nodded to the clerk. "Clear the court!"

Dan and Tom slowly made their way over to Daniel Leake as the pirates shuffled out of the courtroom and were taken back to the stifling gaol in Port Royal, where most of them would be spending their last night on earth.

CHAPTER 16

THE GALLOWS' JIG

The coach bumped along the rutted path to Port Royal. Dan and Tom faced Daniel Leake across the rocking carriage.

"I suppose we owe you our thanks," managed Dan. They were the first words he'd spoken since they'd left the court.

"Sure I only spoke the truth, son."

"The truth didn't help John Eaton and his crew. You must have the governor's ear."

Daniel Leake puffed out his chest. "I like to think I have some influence with Sir Nicholas."

"Then I'd like to ask you a favour."

"Ask away."

"I want you to speak up for Scar. Algernon Lynch."

"I already have. He's not going to hang with the rest tomorrow, is he?"

"No, but he's in prison. If you vouched for him, he could stay with us. He could give you his word not to escape, like Tom did."

Daniel Leake shook his head. "He's not to be trusted.

He's a Negro!"

"He's my friend," snapped Dan, glaring at his father.

"And look where your choice of friends has got you. Within inches of the hangman's noose, that's where. You need to choose your friends more carefully."

"And your relations," muttered Tom.

"He's a good man," said Dan. "I'd trust him with my life. I have done."

"I'll not have a Negro under my roof!"

"What? You've got lots of Negroes under your roof. Ruben, Lily …"

"That's my final word, Dan. I've done what I can for him."

They lapsed into a brooding silence for the rest of the journey.

The town house was big and roomy, the whitewashed outer walls giving some relief from the heat of the day. Daniel Leake had quickly taken his leave, feeling the atmosphere between them even more keenly than Dan. 'Treat the place as your own,' were his parting words. 'I only ask that your friend doesn't leave the house, except in the company of O'Connor.' The supervisor was supposedly there to look after the guests, but they all knew that he was really Tom's gaoler, making sure that he didn't abscond before his adjourned trial.

The boys made hammocks out of sheets and hung them on the veranda. After a year at sea, they found chairs and beds awkward and uncomfortable. A cool breeze blowing in from the ocean made it the most pleasant place in the house.

Tom asked O'Connor for some rum. Dan frowned as the man went to fetch it. "You'd better lay off the drink, Tom. You're not out of trouble yet and you should keep a clear head for thinking."

"Why bother? I've got you to do my thinking for me?"

"I *have* been thinking."

Tom sat up. "And?"

"I think you should lay off the rum."

Tom pulled a face and stretched back out in his hammock. "I'll just have the one then. You have to admit it's been a stressful day. "

"Tomorrow will be more stressful."

"Tomorrow can wait."

"Our friends are going to die tomorrow, in case you've forgotten?"

Tom jumped out of his hammock, his face red and his fists bunched. "Of course I haven't forgotten. But we can't help them so there's no point in remembering. That's why I want the rum!"

"Why can't we help them? We need to keep our heads clear and think."

"We can't help them because they're locked in a cell, surrounded by guards. Mary, Anne and Scar, they might live a while longer, but the rest of them are as good as dead."

"Scar and the girls then. We've got to help them. We need a plan."

"Then plan away," said Tom as O'Connor returned with his rum. "You're the one with the brains. Let me know when you've come up with something." He climbed back into his hammock and swung there with his drink in his hand.

Dan spent the rest of the day racking his brains for a plan. He came up with nothing.

Daniel Leake arrived next morning. "I've got news about your fr... about, Algernon Lynch."

The boys jumped to their feet.

"What is it?" urged Dan.

His father threw his hat carelessly on the sideboard then flopped down in a chair, putting his feet up on the coffee table in front of him. He looked up at Dan. "He's a runaway slave."

Dan bit his lip and stole a glance at Tom. "What's going to happen to him?"

"Apparently his old owner died in debt and his plantation was split up. So they're going to auction Lynch tomorrow, in Kingston."

Dan screwed his eyes shut. This was Scar's worst nightmare. He had to do something. "Buy him!" he blurted out.

"Pardon?"

"Buy him, then set him free."

"Are you serious? A Negro his size would go for over fifty guineas." His voice trailed off as he saw the look on Dan's face.

"I owe him my life," Dan pleaded. "Do it for *me*."

"Well, he would make a strong worker. I might buy him, but I won't free him. It sets a bad example having free blacks running around. The others get uppity."

Dan swallowed the bile rising in his throat, and gripped his hands together to stop them shaking. He'd get nowhere by losing his temper. He kept his voice calm. "I'll need a servant, won't I? If you won't free him then buy him for me."

His father looked at him suspiciously.

"I'd not free him without your permission," said Dan quickly.

Daniel Leake nodded slowly. "I'll see what I can do, but no promises." He got to his feet and picked up his hat. "I have to go. Matters to attend to." He looked closely at Dan. "The executions will be at Gallows Point, two o'clock this afternoon. I'd advise you not to be there."

He spun on his heel and left.

Tom watched the emotions playing on his friend's face. "You're planning to go, aren't you?"

"I have to. I owe them that. Are you coming?"

"To watch them kicking out the last seconds of their lives? I don't think so." Tom tried to hold Dan's eyes but couldn't. He looked down. "Anyway, I'm under house arrest, aren't I? I can't go."

Dan hesitated. He didn't want to be alone at the executions, but he had to be there, hadn't he? He made up his mind. "I'm going," he said, his jaw set and his head nodding to confirm his decision.

"Okay mate, you do what you have to do." Tom shuffled out to the veranda and leant silently against the rail, gazing out to the troubled sea.

Dan stared over the heads of the jostling, excited mob, his eyes fixed on the gibbet. Nine nooses hung there, patiently waiting for necks to fill them. He shuddered.

Pedlars and vendors weaved through the packed square, along with the watch-snatchers and pickpockets that always showed up for an execution.

"Buy my pies. Fresh this morning. Penny a pie."

"Rum punch to get you in the mood for a hanging. Rum punch for sale."

As he looked around, Dan thought he saw Thackeray and McKaig at the back of the square, but they soon disappeared in the swirl of bustling people. His heart lifted slightly, but he didn't try to join them.

The mob suddenly erupted into a mixture of cheers and jeers. Two large carts had appeared at the north end of the square. The pirates, arms bound behind their backs, swayed as they fought to keep their balance in the bouncing vehicles. Red-coated soldiers forced a way through the throng with their muskets.

Some women threw flowers at Calico Jack in the leading cart. Others tossed rotten fruit and the contents of chamber pots at the wretched prisoners. Most of the pirates kept their eyes lowered, heads hanging on stooped shoulders, but Anne Bonny and Mary Read, stood tall and defiant, staring a hatred that stayed the hands of the crowd. Calico Jack smiled and winked at women who giggled and fluttered as he passed.

"Wipe that smile off your face," snarled a guard and knocked Jack's tricorn hat off his head and onto the street. A man darted out from the crowd, snatched it up then disappeared back into the milling throng.

In the rear cart, John Eaton squealed out his innocence to the amused crowd who answered with catcalls and well-aimed pots of excrement. Most of his crew stood limp and mute, accepting their unjust fate and mouthing silent prayers.

The carts shuddered to a halt at the foot of the scaffold. The prisoners tried to look away but their eyes were drawn inexorably to the dangling nooses that waited for them. John Eaton's britches darkened as his bladder emptied, and he stood whimpering like a child as the laughing mob taunted him.

Dan watched helplessly as the guards roughly pushed the prisoners out of the carts. Some jumped down to land on their feet but others sprawled painfully on the ground where they fell. The viewing gallery for the wealthier citizens had filled up now, and the crowd quietened as Sir Nicholas Lawes took his seat. They looked expectantly at the governor.

"Carry on," he said with a wave of his hand and the crowd cheered as John Eaton and his crew were forced up the scaffold steps at bayonet point.

The fat hangman rammed a noose over each of their heads, his fleshy jowls quivering as he called out their names and crimes.

"John Howard - Pirate!"

The fisherman shook uncontrollably as he felt the rope on his neck. "But I'm innocent," he pleaded. "I'm innocent!"

"John Henson – Pirate!"

John Henson winced as the noose was forced down over the raw hole where his left ear used to be. He'd lost it when Mary Read had fired her pistols through the cabin door when they'd been captured. He felt a stab of envy for his friend who had taken her other shot between the eyes. This was one party he'd have been glad to miss.

"Edward Warner - Pirate! Thomas Baker – Pirate!" The hangman paused, enjoying his work. "Benjamin Palmer – Pirate!"

The thirteen-year-old boy began to sob quietly as the hangman waved the noose in front of his eyes.

The fat man grinned, malice shining from his close-set, piggy eyes. "Piss yourself if you want. The crowd always enjoys that. You'll be pissing and shitting your britches anyway once we hoist you up."

The boy turned pale and set up a low moaning sound that cut through Dan like an ice sword.

"John Cole – Pirate! Walter Rouse – Pirate! Thomas Quick – Pirate!"

Thomas Quick could hardly stand, blood crusted on the bandage on the festering stump where his arm had been. His other arm was tied tightly to his side.

"John Eaton– Pirate!"

"I'm not a pirate," cried the small man, shaking his head violently from side to side, trying to stop the noose from being placed around his neck. "I'm not with them. I'm not with them!"

The crowd roared with laughter and pelted him with rotten fruit.

With the last of the nooses in place, the hangman

lumbered over to the lever for the trapdoors. The Anglican minister took a surreptitious sip from his hip-flask then moved along the line of quaking men, slurring words of comfort and blessing those who repented their sins. His work done he swayed to the back of the gallows.

"I'm not one of them! I'm not a pirate... not a pirate." John Eaton's cries fell to a pathetic whimper.

On the viewing platform, the governor raised his arm and the drums began beating out the final heartbeats of the men on the gibbet. His arm dropped and the drums fell instantly silent. The hangman hauled back on the lever.

Dan kept his eyes on the ground but heard the bang of falling trapdoors then a sickening ripple of cracks as necks snapped at the end of the drop. He looked up and saw nine bodies, some still twitching, swaying on the ends of the ropes, dark steaming patches showing where the dead men's bladders and bowels had emptied.

The crowd cheered and the drink vendors doubled their custom.

Guards lowered the bodies from the gibbet, and night-soil men carted them away to be buried face down in unconsecrated ground, facing hell not heaven.

While the gallows was being reset, the pirates waited, offering half-forgotten prayers to a god most of them didn't believe in. Finally it was ready and nine more men made the weary climb up the scaffold.

The hangman began his routine, placing nooses around necks and calling out the names of the condemned.

"John Howell – Pirate! Thomas Earl – Pirate! Patrick Carty – Pirate!"

Patrick Carty winced from the pain in his injured leg, but didn't fight the noose as the hangman rammed it over his head.

"James Dobbin – Pirate! Noah Harwood –Pirate! Richard Corner – Pirate."

"Get on with it!" called out a woman. The crowd was growing restless, eager for blood.

"Don't rush me, ladies. You like gentlemen to be well hung, don't you?"

The mob laughed and the hangman grinned. He'd won them back again.

"Thomas Bourn, alias Brown – the colour his britches are going to be in a minute. Pirate."

The crowd guffawed again. The hangman was warming to his task.

"John Fenwick." He pretended to do a double take, staring at the portly old sailor. "I think I'll need a thicker rope for you. You'll snap this one like a twig." The cackling crowd were lapping it up. "Pirate!"

Dan had his head down, unconsciously wringing his hands together, dreading the next name to be called out.

"George Featherston – Pirate!"

Dan swallowed hard and looked up. The bosun stood unmoving as the hangman placed the noose around his thick neck, his unblinking eyes staring straight ahead, ignoring the baying mob beneath him. As the drums started again, Dan tore his eyes away. They fell silent and he tensed, his ears straining for the sound he didn't want to hear. Then it came. The thud of trapdoors falling from under the pirates, followed by the rippling crack of

183

breaking necks.

The crowd whooped with delight, but this time it was different. The shouting and laughter went on and on. Dan forced his eyes open. Eight men hung limp on the end of their ropes but one still kicked and bucked, his strong neck straining against the choking noose. It was George Featherston.

The mob cheered him on as he kicked out his life at the end of the rope. Some sang sea-shanties to accompany his mad dance as, eyes bulging, he slowly choked to death.

The governor took pity on him and ordered the reluctant hangman to hurry the end. The fat executioner, scowling behind his flabby cheeks, climbed slowly down the scaffold then jumped up and hung onto the bosun's legs, waving to the screeching crowd as he swung back and forth, a giant, malevolent toad, fastened to its victim. The sight sickened Dan to the stomach but the extra weight put a mercifully swift end to his friend who finally hung limp and silent from the gibbet.

The hangman started back up the gallows but stopped to leer at the two women. "You're too light, my dears. Your necks won't snap. You'll be dancing away like your friend there. Twenty minutes a-piece I reckon."

Mary Read looked him straight in the eye then spat in his face. Calico Jack laughed out loud.

The scowling hangman shuffled up the steps muttering, "You'll not be laughing soon, shipmate. We've got something special planned for you."

Only four prisoners remained now: Mary Read, Anne Bonny, Calico Jack, and John Davis who sprawled on a stretcher, his broken legs unset. At a nod from the governor, two soldiers carried the stretcher up the steps. They dropped it at the top and pulled the writhing pirate out. As they dragged his smashed legs across the gallows floor he stifled a scream that came out as a high-pitched hiss. A noose was placed around his neck and the soldiers held him while the hangman dropped the trapdoor under him. He dangled over the opening, pinioned between the two men, his breath coming in ragged gasps. Sir Nicholas Lawes dropped his arm and the redcoats dropped John Davis through the opening. There was a loud crack as the rope sprung tight, snapping his neck. The crowd roared their approval.

As Dan watched, Anne Bonny, Mary Read and Calico Jack strode gamely up the scaffold determined to show no fear. The drums started to roll but Sir Nicholas stood and held up his hand for silence.

The drums stopped.

The governor drew himself up to his full height and addressed the prisoners. "Anne Bonny and Mary Read. You are pirates, murderesses, thieves and worse, but I have decided to show clemency for the sake of your unborn children. You will not be hanged until after they are born. They will be taken away and raised by good Christians, and then you will face the gallows for your crimes."

He turned his cold eyes on Calico Jack. "But you, John Rackham, can expect no mercy. You will be hanged and disembowelled then your body tarred and chained, and left to swing over the harbour until it rots. Let this serve as an example to any young men or women who might otherwise wish to follow in your footsteps. May The Lord have mercy on your soul."

Anne Bonny turned on Calico Jack, whose head and shoulders had slumped on hearing his dreadful fate. "I'm sorry, Jack," she said fiercely, "but if you had fought like a man you would not now be about to die like a dog. Do straighten yourself up."

Slowly, Calico Jack raised his head and pulled back his shoulders. Taking a deep breath he addressed the crowd in a strong, steady voice, admitting his crimes and submitting himself to God's mercy, then stepped under the noose. As it was placed around his neck he caught Dan's eyes, and he winked and gave a sad smile.

As the drums began their final roll, Dan turned and ran from the dockside. The date was the 18th November 1720. It was his 16th birthday.

CHAPTER 17

GAOLBREAK

Tom had just heard the fate of his shipmates and he paced the room, his face an angry scowl. "There's no justice in this world. Not for the likes of us there isn't. Only for the rich."

"They even executed John Eaton and his crew," added Dan, shaking his head. "There was no proof they'd committed a crime, but they hanged them anyway! They had more reason to hang you and me, but we're alive and they're dead."

"Because your father's rich," said Tom.

"Yeah," spat Dan. "Because my father's rich." He looked around the expensively furnished room. "I wish I'd died with them!"

"Don't say that, Dan!"

"I thought I was being brave, not signing the *Articles*, but I wasn't. I was being a coward. When I found out my father wasn't... wasn't the man I thought... I should have signed on then. I should have realised that that ship was my home; that the crew were my friends and family. I should have taken my chances; lived or died with them.

Well now they're dead and I wish I was."

The sound of a carriage pulling up jolted them from their thoughts. The door opened and Daniel Leake breezed in.

"I've a surprise for you, Dan," he smiled, pleased with himself.

"What is it?" Dan stared out the window, his voice flat and monotone.

"Algernon Lynch. I've bought him!"

Dan spun around. "Scar?" He nearly threw his arms around his father but stopped just short. "Thank you! Thank you! Thank you!" The words gushed out.

Tom was on his feet, clapping Dan on the back.

Daniel Leake beamed at his son.

Dan bounced up and down on his toes. "When can I see him?"

"Not until he's been broken."

Dan stood very still. "What do you mean, 'broken'?"

"He's been free too long," said Daniel Leake, pouring himself a drink from a decanter on the sideboard. "Living as a pirate! Free from even the bonds of society. He'll need breaking before he can become a personal slave to a young gentleman. I'm having him whipped in the morning."

"What?"

"And every morning for a week — or however long it takes to break his spirit."

Dan glared at his father, loathing in his voice. "You'll never break his spirit."

"Then he's in for a short and very painful life."

Dan gave a strangled cry and fled from the room.

Daniel Leake shrugged. "What's the matter with him?"

"Nothing I can think of," snarled Tom, and set off after his friend.

Tom's eyes widened as he stared at Dan. "You're not serious are you?"

"I'm not going to sit here and let Scar be whipped. And I'll not witness any more of my friends executed — not unless I hang with them." Dan put his hand on Tom's shoulder. "Are you with me? I can't do this on my own."

"Of course I'm with you. Just because you've lost the plot doesn't mean I'm not with you."

"Give O'Connor the slip then. Find McKaig and Thackeray. I saw them at the hangings. They're around somewhere. They'll be holed up in some alehouse. Tell them to get a crew together and to keep an eye out for a likely ship to steal. Something small and fast."

Tom looked troubled. "But I gave my word I wouldn't try to escape."

"Break it," snapped Dan. "We owe these people nothing." He paced up and down as he talked, his brain whirling. "Make sure you're in The Three Horseshoes every evening at nine. I'll meet you there when I can."

"And when's that likely to be?" asked Tom.

"I have to get Scar out tonight, before he's flogged. I can manage that."

"And the girls?"

"I don't know how or when, but I'll get them out."

Tom scratched his head. "You do know they're in gaol,

don't you? Locked doors, guards, that sort of thing?"

"The gaol's no longer full of dangerous pirates, just two friendless, pregnant women. I'm betting there'll be no soldiers there now; just the gaoler and maybe a couple of his bullyboys. They'll not be expecting any trouble."

"Are you sure you don't want me to come with you?"

"I need you in Port Royal, Tom. I want a ship and a crew lined up and ready to go when I get Anne and Mary out. Without that we'll be caught in no time. Find Thackeray and McKaig. I'm relying on you."

"I won't let you down." Tom held out his hand. "Good luck!"

Dan took it and shook it warmly, then disappeared into the night.

The Yallahs road was dark but the moon dripped enough light through the scudding clouds for Dan to see his way. The wind blew his hair back from his face as he reached his father's plantation. As he moved to the gate, a low growling came from the other side and he prayed the dogs would remember him. He called to them soothingly and produced two pieces of pork that he'd taken from the larder at the town house. The wolfhounds accepted his bribe with wagging tails, and gulped down the meat. Judging it was safe he climbed tentatively over the locked gate.

The dogs nudged him, wanting more food. "Sorry boys. That's all I had on me," whispered Dan, stroking the thick fur on their backs. They padded alongside as he made his way silently towards the slave quarters.

At the back of the house stood two large, barn-like

structures, one for the male slaves and one for the females. Between them squatted a small but sturdy, padlocked shack. Dan took a guess and put an ear to the door. He could hear slow, rhythmic breathing.

"Scar," he whispered, then louder, "Scar!"

He heard someone stirring inside. "That you, Dan?" came a booming whisper.

"Yeah, it's me." In his excitement, Dan struggled to keep his voice low. "I'm going to get you out. Do you know where the key is?"

He leapt back as Scar's huge shoulder appeared, the door swinging off its hinges. "Don't need key!"

The dogs began to growl but Dan quietened them, tickling their ears. They sniffed tentatively at Scar. "That wasn't very clever," he hissed at the giant. "You might have been heard!" But no lights or sound came from the big house.

"You have plan?" asked Scar in the nearest thing to a whisper he could manage. "Where do we go?"

"Gaol." said Dan.

"Gaol!"

"Shh! We're going to break out Anne and Mary."

Scar's big head nodded slowly. "Now?"

"Right now. When they realise you've escaped and I've gone missing, they'll put two and two together and guess that I'm involved. I want to get them out before that happens. Let's go."

"Wait," said Scar. "Free other slaves before go."

"We can't!" gasped Dan. "I mean... how many of them are there?"

"Eighty."

"Eighty! We can't escape with eighty slaves."

"How plan get off island?" asked Scar.

"We'll steal a ship."

Scar's eyes were bright in the moonlight as the clouds moved out to sea leaving a clear night sky. "Need crew then."

"I'm planning to steal a sloop, not a ruddy galleon! Anyway, Tom's sorting out a crew."

"Jack not have luck with that," said Scar. "Why Tom more successful?"

"I... I don't know. But eighty's too many." Dan's eyes darted round to the house. "And we need to get out of here!"

Scar stood his ground. "They not all come. They scare. Some stay, some run."

Dan hesitated and Scar marched over to the nearest slave block. The door wasn't even locked. He pushed it open and stepped inside. Female voices called out. "Who's there? What you want?"

Scar hushed them. "We break out. Who come with us?"

The silence dragged on for minutes then a lone voice answered him. "Where you take us? Where we go?"

"We sail off island," said Scar.

"You got ship?"

"Gonna steal one."

"Gonna get yourself killed, that what you gonna do."

"Better die free than live slave!"

"We got pickney here," said one of the women. "We want to live."

Scar's voice dropped so low that Dan could barely hear the words. "No-one come? No-one?"

Silence greeted his question.

"Let's go," said Dan, pulling on Scar's arm. The big man reluctantly followed him out.

"Come on!" hissed Dan as Scar paused by the male slave block. This one was locked. "We've wasted enough time."

Scar grunted as he snapped off the padlock with his bare hands. The noise started the occupants awake and they stared, wide-eyed, at the two intruders who stepped through the doorway.

"We break out," said Scar. "We have ship. Who come?"

Again, silence. Then, "You know what they do to runaway slaves?"

"Yes," said Scar bleakly. "If catch them."

"I'm with you," called a voice. Then another and another. Half-a-dozen men came to the doorway. The rest remained crouching in the hut, terrified of what fate might lie ahead, beyond that open door.

Scar shook his head in anger and disappointment as he ushered the six men out. "If anyone warn boss, Scar come back. Burn hut down with all in it."

The slaves eyed the huge figure filling the doorway, and said nothing. They'd be beaten when the breakout was discovered, but they'd live. They'd remain quiet until the morning.

The dogs followed them down the path, their tails wagging as Dan gave them a final pat before following

Scar and the others over the gate. They turned towards Port Royal and hurried along the road.

"So, what are we meant to do with this lot?" grumbled Dan, pointing at the six runaways. "We can't just walk up to the gaol with them in tow."

Scar didn't break stride. "Tell gaoler slave escape and Dan catch."

Dan looked around at the burly slaves and back at Scar. "Yeah, right! Me bring you lot in, armed with only a knife? I don't think so."

"Dan think of something," said Scar, marching on down the road.

"Thanks!" said Dan, pulling his jacket tighter around him and following after the others. *Why do I have to be the one to think of something?* He rubbed the back of his neck and racked his brain as they trudged on.

When they reached the outskirts of Port Royal, Dan led them off the road and into the shadows. "My father has a warehouse on the waterfront," he told Scar. "He stores sugar and molasses there. It's not due to be shipped out for a while so it might be a good place for us to hole up. He won't expect his runaway slaves to be hiding in his own property."

The giant grinned in the moonlight. "Scar said Dan think of something."

They crept through the quayside, keeping away from lights and the sound of people. Dan brought them to a halt outside a large building fronting the harbour. "This is it."

He tried the front entrance, but the heavy doors wouldn't budge. The small, inset proved equally stubborn.

They moved around the warehouse until one of the slaves grabbed Dan's arm and pointed up. A window hung open, high in the side of the building. Dan looked at it dubiously. "*You* might be able to reach it Scar, but you'd never fit through!"

Without a word, Scar hoisted Dan off his feet and propelled him up to the window.

"I'll see you back at the doors," whispered Dan.

He crawled through the window and perched on the ledge, peering into the black nothingness on the other side. He edged down, holding on to the sill, his knuckles white as his feet dangled over the dark void. He mumbled a quick prayer, the sweat on his hands already loosening his grip on the ledge, then he dropped into the darkness.

His feet hit the floor and he tumbled sideways on bent knees, silently thanking George Featherston. 'Anyone who goes up in the rigging needs to know how to fall,' he'd insisted. Dan's throat tightened as he thought of the bosun and how he'd died.

He put his hands out in front of him and found the wall, following it around until he came to the warehouse doors. A little moonlight shone in round the edges of the frame, and he could hear Scar and the others outside. His groping hands found the wooden locking bar, and he lifted it out of its hooks. The doors swung open emitting a little light as Scar led the runaways inside. The big man waited at the open doors while Dan took them into the depths.

"Stay here and don't move," he told them. "We'll be back with food and drink when we can. One of you bar the doors after us."

Dan hurried to join Scar in the street.

A single light shone from the gaol house. Dan peered through the barred window. The gaoler dozed in a chair, a guttering candle on the table in front of him. Beside the candle sat a large set of keys and what remained of the gaoler's supper.

"How many man?" whispered Scar.

"Only one, I think," said Dan, stealing round to try the door. It was locked. He moved back to the window. "Hey, Gaoler!"

The fat man's eyes flickered open. "What? Who is it? Who's there?"

"Dan Leake. I need to talk to Anne Bonny."

"Clear off!" barked the gaoler. "Come back in the morning."

Dan reached into his pocket and pulled out a coin. He held it up to window. "There's a gold sovereign in it for you if I can see her tonight."

The gaoler's piggy eyes opened wider. He struggled to his feet and waddled over to the window. "Give it here!" he demanded, holding out a podgy hand.

"Not until you let me in."

The fat man shook his head but kept his eyes on the money. "Two sovereigns," he said. "One now and one when I open the door."

Dan nodded, handed over the coin and made his way to the front of the gaol. Keys jangled on the other side of the door, then it swung open. The gaoler appeared, holding out his hand again. Dan passed over the second coin.

The gaoler grinned maliciously as he pocketed the money. "Now clear off or you'll get my boot up yer hole!"

"Oh dear," said Dan. "It'll have to be Plan B then."

"Plan B?"

Scar's massive fist flew out of the dark. The fat man's feet left the ground and he crashed, unconscious, to the floor.

"Quick! Get him inside," said Dan, eyes darting around. But nothing stirred in the courtyard.

Dan shut the door behind them, took the keys then hurried into the building.

"Anne? Mary?" he whispered from cell to cell.

At last a reply came. "Dan? Is that you? What's happening?"

It was Anne Bonny.

"I'm getting you out," said Dan. "Where's Mary?"

"Dead!"

Dan froze. "What do you mean, 'dead'?"

"The fever took her." Anne's voice rose in anger. "That puff-gutted muck-spout of a gaoler wouldn't fetch a doctor. Mary's dead."

Dan stood for a moment, his head lowered.

"Don't just stand there," hissed Anne. "Get me out!"

Fumbling with the keys, Dan finally got the right one and unlocked the door. Anne barged past him. He hurried back the way he'd come and found her viciously kicking the unconscious gaoler.

"For pity's sake, keep quiet!" He grabbed her and tried to pull her away.

She broke free, stamping down. "That's for Mary, you

murdering–"

Scar's huge hand clamped over her mouth. He plucked her from her feet and carried her, squirming and kicking, through the doorway. Dan scooped up a wine skin and some bread and cheese from the table, then followed them out. "This way," he said and led Scar, who still carried his struggling captive, from the square.

Anne stopped struggling as they reached the darkness of a nearby alley.

"If he lets you go will you keep quiet?" whispered Dan.

She nodded and Scar lowered her to the ground. "I'm sorry," she said. "But that murdering pig had it coming."

"I know how you feel," said Dan. "But we've got to get out of here. It's not just *our* lives depending on it."

Dan led them down a series of winding alleys to the quayside, and sought out the warehouse. Scar called quietly. A few seconds later, the door inched open and they ducked inside.

The runaways gulped down the wine Dan had brought. "Take it easy," he said. "That has to last us — I don't know how long."

He turned to Anne Bonny. "This is our new crew."

"Then Lord help us!" said Anne, screwing up her nose. She faced Dan. "So we're taking a ship, are we? We'll not sail her with this lot."

"Tom's out looking for Thackeray and McKaig. They'll find us sailors. These men can provide the muscle as they learn the ropes."

"Hmm…"

"All started somewhere," rumbled Scar.

"So we did," said Anne. "But if we're going to get out of here we'll need to sail and fight hard and fast. They can't sail and they can't fire a cannon."

"You do sail. Scar teach fire cannon," said the big man. "And they fight. They fight like demons. Not go back to hell that wait them if capture."

They hid out in the warehouse all day then, as night fell, Dan left to keep his appointment with Tom. The Three Horseshoes was quiet with only a few old drunks sitting around. Dan spotted Tom at a table in a dark corner. He faced the door, his back to the wall. Dan smiled to himself. They were both learning.

"Well?" Tom raised an eyebrow, putting down his tankard of ale.

"Piece of cake," said Dan, smiling.

Tom frowned, studying his friend's face to see if he was making fun of him. "You got Scar and the girls out?"

Dan's smile slipped. "Scar and Anne, yes." He paused. "Mary's dead."

"She's what?"

"She's dead, Tom."

Tom slumped and lowered his head, staring fixedly at the table. "How... How did it happen?"

"Fever. The gaoler wouldn't send for a doctor."

Tom looked up, his eyes red-rimmed. "The gaoler, is he still alive?"

Dan nodded. "He's alive."

Tom's eyes narrowed to twin slits but his voice stayed chillingly flat. "Good," he said quietly. "I want to watch him as he dies."

Dan sat down by his friend. "You've got to leave it, Tom. You have to think of the rest of us. If you go charging about after the gaoler we could all end up dead."

A pained silence dragged on until Tom finally spoke. "I found Thackeray and McKaig. They're getting a crew together. That will leave me a night or two to do what I have to do."

"No, Tom. Promise me you won't go near him."

"Sorry Dan, I can't do that." Tom straightened, a vein pulsing in his neck. "I'll wait until you've got a crew and picked out a ship, then I'm going to kill him. If I'm not back in time, sail without me."

"Tom!"

"He's going to die. End of story."

Dan looked into his friend's eyes and knew there was no point in arguing further. He sighed and pushed back his chair. "Have you brought any food?"

Tom passed over a bag with some bread and cheese in it.

"That's not going to go far," said Dan, frowning. "There are nine of us."

"Nine?"

"When you see Thackeray and McKaig, tell them that I've got six new crewmen for them."

"Sailors?"

"Well, no. They're runaway slaves, but they'll work hard, and they'll fight. They've got to be better than nothing."

"McKaig wouldn't agree with you. He's been turning

down landlubbers all day. Says it's hard enough for a sailor to do his own job without having to nursemaid some farmhand or clerk."

"McKaig wouldn't agree with his own mother. Those men are coming with us whether he likes it or not."

"Runaways will bring the authorities down on us, Dan. They'll be out in force looking for them."

"And you killing the gaoler won't bring them down on us?" Tom closed his mouth and Dan went on. "They'll be searching the hills for them. They won't expect runaway slaves to seize a ship. I mean, who'd navigate?"

Tom looked hard at him. "That's another thing. Who *will* navigate?"

"I will."

"You?"

"Why not? George Featherston was teaching me. If I can get some charts, a back-staff, a compass and an hourglass, I'll be fine."

"Somehow you're not filling me with confidence, Dan."

"I can do it. Would you rather stay here?"

"No. I'm with you. You know that. I'd just rather have a captain who knows his arse from his elbow."

"Thanks. I'll tell you what. We'll kidnap a navigator the first chance we get, if that makes you happier."

"Believe me it does."

"That will be our first act of piracy then," said Dan, holding out his hand.

Tom looked at the hand, then at Dan's face. "So we're turning pirate, are we? You've changed your tune?"

"I've had enough of 'honest' men to last me a lifetime.

201

I've come to realise that justice and the law are two different things. I've been forced to choose and I've chosen justice."

Tom took the outstretched hand and shook it warmly. "To be honest mate, I don't know the difference. But it's gonna be fun."

CHAPTER 18

THE PIRATE CAPTAIN

After a sleepless night and a long, hungry day, Dan rejoined Tom in The Three Horseshoes. Thackeray and McKaig were with him. His heart lifted when he saw the two old pirates, but there was no time for small talk. "How many men have you found?" he asked them.

"There's us four, Scar and Anne. That makes... six," said Thackeray counting them out on his fingers, eyes screwed tight in concentration. "And we've got twelve new sailors signed on. All good men with no respect for the law. That makes... um." Thackeray looked puzzled. He'd run out of fingers.

Dan helped him out. "Eighteen."

"Eighteen. That's what I said. And you?"

"Six."

"Are they seamen or lubbers?" grunted McKaig.

Dan hesitated, watching the Scotsman's face. "They're runaway slaves!"

"Six more," said Thackeray, oblivious to his friend's rising colour and temper. "So that's... eighteen plus six."

"Ye cannae count *them*," shouted McKaig. "They're no'

sailors. They'll be useless."

"You're useless but I counted you," snapped Thackeray.

"You'll be useless after I get hold of ye," growled McKaig, pushing himself up from the table.

"Eighteen's more than enough to sail a ship," Dan interrupted before the two old sea-dogs could come to blows. "And we'll have six extra fighting men on board. They're not afraid of hard work, and they can learn the ropes as they go."

McKaig fumed for a minute then muttered, "Well, it's against my advice," as he raised his tankard and emptied it in one go.

Dan turned his attention back to Thackeray. "Where are these twelve men of yours then?"

"They're in The Skull and Crossbones. I didn't want to raise suspicion by having us all meeting up in one place."

"Right," said Dan. "Good idea. Have you picked out a ship for us yet?"

"I have." Thackeray's wrinkled face lit up. "She's the finest brig you've ever clapped eyes on. She'll sail like a dream."

"Humph! Tell him the rest!" grunted McKaig.

"There's no one on board. They're all in town getting drunk."

"That's perfect!" Dan, jumped his feet. "What are we waiting for? We'll not get a better chance than this!"

McKaig stayed where he was. "Tell him the name of the ship."

Thackeray glared at the one-legged pirate. "She's the *Fortune*."

"So what?" said Dan.

McKaig got up from the table and moved his mouth close to Dan's ear. "So, she's one of Black Bart's ships, that's what."

"Black Bart?" Dan paled a little.

"That's why they havenae bothered to leave anyone on board. No-one's stupid enough to steal one of Black Bart's ships."

"That's where you're wrong," said Dan, brightening up. "We are!"

McKaig took a step back. "Are ye mad? At least Thackeray's got an excuse. He's senile. What's yours? Black Bart hanged the governor of Martinique from the yard-arm of that ship. What dae ye think he'll dae tae us if he catches us? Thanks to you we'll have the slavers after us as well as the Admiralty. But neither will get anywhere near us if we take that ship. Coz Black Bart will catch us first and nail us to the mast by our gingamobs."

"But he won't have a ship will he? So how can he catch us?"

"That's not his main ship," said McKaig. "His flagship's the *Royal Fortune*. She's being refitted at the moment. She's bigger, faster and more heavily armed than the *Fortune*."

"Well if she's being refitted, that gives us a head start," said Dan with a calm he didn't feel. "We'll get out of these waters. Sail for North America or Africa. Yes, Africa. We could prey on the slave-ships. Take their goods before they can trade them for slaves. We'd be doing the world a service and making ourselves rich at the same time."

"We'll be making ourselves dead!" barked McKaig. "Interfere with the slave-trade and we'll have half of Europe after our blood, not just Black Bart. And he'll no' stop until he's butchered us all."

"You stay here then, if yer yellow," sneered Thackeray.

"I didnae say I wasnae coming. I just said yer both mad, and ye are!"

"Let's go then. We're wasting valuable time," said Dan, and they followed him out into the night.

Thackeray and McKaig went to collect their men from The Skull and Crossbones while Dan and Tom picked up Scar and the others. They met up on the waterfront and Dan questioned Thackeray.

"There she is," said the old pirate, pointing out into the harbour.

A sleek-looking brig bobbed in the moonlight, a single stern lanthorn picking out her name, *Fortune*.

A line of rowing boats nestled at the pontoon beneath them. "Quick, into the boats," said Dan.

"Wait!" Tom stood apart from the others. "There's something I have to do."

"Please, Tom. Forget the gaoler. Come with us now."

No emotion showed on Tom's hard-set face. "It won't take long. I'll catch you up when I can. Don't wait for me."

Dan could do nothing as his friend disappeared into the maze of alleys. They boarded the nearest two boats, Dan taking the tiller of one, and Anne Bonny the other. They slipped their moorings and dipped their oars into the inky water, rowing stealthily towards the *Fortune*.

Checking the knife in his belt, Dan crept up the ship's side, the rest of the crew following. He peered over the rail. It seemed that Thackeray was right. There was no one aboard. They eased themselves onto the deck.

"Scar," whispered Dan. "Take your men and search below. Thackeray, McKaig, you check the fo'c'sle. If there's any trouble, that's where we'll find it. Take the sailors with you. And send someone up to the crow's nest. Make sure there's no lookout dozing up there."

"I'll check the quarterdeck," said Anne Bonny, moving toward the stern.

"Right," said Dan. "I'll be in the cabin looking for charts."

They split up and spread silently around the ship. Dan slipped into the grand cabin. The waning moon filtered in through the stern windows giving him some light to search by. He froze, sure that he'd heard a faint noise. In the stillness he could make out Anne Bonny's footsteps on the quarterdeck above. He relaxed and moved to the big desk opposite the door. A smile spread over his face. A chart lay open on the desktop and others were piled up beside it. He tried the drawers one by one. In the third he found what he was looking for. Rutters. The books where Black Bart would have noted the tides, currents, trade winds, shoals, reefs and so on, that he'd encountered on his voyages. George Featherston had told him these were essential for any navigator in strange waters.

As he placed the rutters on the desk he sensed movement behind him. Before he could turn, a powerful hand shot out and grabbed him by the shoulder.

"Got you thief!" rasped a voice that chilled Dan to the marrow. "You'll regret the day you stole from Black Bart!"

The hand spun him around and Dan caught a quick glimpse of a huge, shaggy-haired man in a nightshirt, before a ham-sized fist slammed into the side of his head and sent him crashing over the desk to the floor.

"Now, where's my sword?" he heard above the ringing in his ears. "Ah, there you are my beauty."

The chilling rasp of a sword being drawn from its scabbard reached his ears then heavy footsteps came around the desk. Dan scrambled away from the noise, shaking his throbbing head, trying desperately to clear it.

"I see you, thief. I'm gonna chop you to pieces and feed you to the sharks."

The light from the stern windows silhouetted the big man as he raised his sword over Dan, who lay semi-dazed, mesmerised by the sight of his coming death.

"Black Bart says hello," growled the pirate. "And goodbye!"

The cabin door burst open as the blade began to slash down, and Anne Bonny flung herself into the room. Dan rolled despairingly to the side and the sword cut harmlessly into the floor as Black Bart dashed his gaze towards the door.

Anne Bonny took in the scene in a second and threw herself onto the man's back, one hand at his throat and the other clawing for his eyes. He let out a howl of pain and hurled her against the wall. A sickening crash echoed around the cabin as she slid, limp and bleeding, to the floor.

"Two thieves," Black Bart muttered as he yanked his sword from the planks of the floor.

He ambled over to Anne Bonny, taking his time. Dan could feel his head starting to clear, his senses coming back. The pirate was only feet from him, his sword pointing at Anne who lay on the floor.

"Nobody steals from Black Bart, and lives."

Dan fumbled for the hilt of his knife, and his hand finally closed around it.

Black Bart drew back his sword arm. "Die!" he yelled.

Dan lunged and drove the dagger into the pirate's leg with all his might. Black Bart let out a scream of pain and rage, swinging his sword back-handed at Dan who ducked under it and rolled to his feet, swaying slightly.

Dan moved backwards away from Anne, drawing the pirate captain with him, his accent coming out now his blood was up. "Come on ye Gom. Scared of a little knife, are yez? Come and fight me."

"An Irishman," screamed Black Bart, hacking wildly. Again he missed as Dan ducked and weaved in the semi-darkness.

Footsteps pounded across the deck and down the companionway.

"Ha!" cried Black Bart. "My crew's returned. Drop your knife, thief!"

"That's *my* crew," said Dan coldly. "You can drop your sword or keep it. Either way I'm going to kill you!"

"Who *are* you?" The pirate captain moved away from the door and the pounding footsteps, edging towards the stern. "Whoever you are, I'll find you." He flung open a window. "I'll find you and I'll destroy you. No-one steals from Black Bart and lives to tell the tale."

Dan took a step towards him.

"I'll destroy you!" yelled the pirate, hurling his cutlass through the air.

Dan leapt to the side and the sword buried itself in the wall.

As Scar and the others barrelled into the room, Black Bart threw himself out into the dark waters of the harbour.

Thackeray ran to the window and stared after the man swimming strongly for the dockside. "Who was that?"

Dan joined him. "That was Back Bart."

He noticed a rowing boat heading towards them, and prayed it was Tom.

"Black Bart? And you're still alive?"

"Only just. Anne saved me. Anne!" He scrambled over to where she lay by the wall.

"I'm alright," he heard her say quietly. "Just a little shaken. Is Dan okay?"

"It's me, Anne. I'm fine, thanks to you." He reached down and hugged her to him.

"This is all very touching," said McKaig. "But I'm thinking we should be getting underway afore Black Bart returns with his crew."

Dan reluctantly left Anne in the hands of one of the new men, Ben Wickham, a barber by trade and therefore used to doctoring. "Thackeray, you're bosun now. Take the sailors and get the ship underway."

"Hang on!" butted in McKaig. "Who made *you* captain?"

"Can *you* navigate, McKaig?"

"Well no, but…"

"Can any of you?"

McKaig stuck his gnarled face in Dan's. "I'll no' have a wee skit o' a lad as my captain."

"We'll vote on it later," snapped Dan. "Right now we need to get going."

Tom appeared in the doorway, flushed and bloody.

Dan moved towards him. "Are you hurt?"

"It's not my blood," said Tom.

Dan crossed himself, took a deep breath, and then pressed on. "Tom, take charge of the topmen. Get the sails up. Scar, take your men and raise the anchor."

Tom led the new topmen up into the rigging and unfurled the canvas in the dark. Scar encouraged the runaways as they toiled at the capstan, raising the heavy anchor, while Thackeray stamped around the ship shouting orders. Anne Bonny stood by Dan at the helm, ready to take the brig out of the harbour.

When the stubborn anchor at last came free, the topmen sheeted in the sails and the ship eased forward on the light wind. As the brig left the shelter of the harbour she heeled over, the sea-breeze filling her sails.

Anne Bonny called the crew together. "We need to vote in a new captain. I say Dan Leake. Who's with me?"

The escaped slaves looked to Scar.

"Dan," he thundered.

"Dan," they echoed.

The new men hesitated as McKaig shouted, "We can do

better than him."

Scar plucked McKaig from the deck and hoisted him high above his head. He marched to the rail and held him over the black ocean. "Who *you* vote for?"

"I… I dinnae…"

Scar pretended to drop the squealing Scotsman then caught him again. "Who you vote for?"

"Dan," squeaked McKaig. "I vote Dan Leake!"

Scar scowled at the rest of the crew, and they wilted under his baleful glare. "Dan," they called. "Dan Leake."

Scar lowered the cursing Scotsman to the deck.

"Right," said Dan. "Anne Bonny will be Ship's Master. Thackeray will be Bosun. Scar, you'll be Gun Captain. Ben Wickham, Surgeon. Tom, you're First Mate."

"And what about *me*, laddie. If ye think…"

"You'll be Quartermaster, Mister McKaig."

"Dinnae bother trying tae…" The Scotsman paused in mid-flight. "Quartermaster?"

"That's right," said Dan. "Quartermaster. In charge of food, rum, and all other provisions. And the division of spoils."

"Aye," said McKaig, a slow smile spreading over his weather-beaten face. "That might be acceptable. That might just be acceptable." With that, he disappeared below to 'check' the stocks of rum and food.

Dan turned to Thackeray. "What about you. I noticed you didn't vote."

"Wait there a minute." The old pirate rummaged in his knapsack then pulled out a battered tricorn hat. "This was Calico Jack's," he said gravely. "Now it's yours." He reverentially straightened out the hat then placed it on Dan's head. "Where away, Captain?" he cried.

Dan looked back at the rapidly disappearing lights of Jamaica. "Away from here," he said quietly. "Well away from here."

He pulled the silver locket from around his neck and opened it, staring one last time at his father's portrait. With an oath, he snapped it shut and hurled it out into the churning ocean.

The ship's company watched him in silence, and Dan realised they were waiting for orders. His orders. He straightened up and raised his voice. "Clear the quarterdeck! Helmsman, bring us closer to the wind. Topmen, trim those sails."

The crew jumped to their duties and the ship skipped over the waves, racing out into the welcoming night.

"And, Tom." Dan smiled as his friend turned to him. "Hoist the Black Flag!"

***

HISTORICAL NOTE

While Dan, Tom, Scar, Thackeray and McKaig are fictional, many of the other characters in the book are real historical figures and many of the events described did actually occur.

THE PIRATES

Anne Bonny, Mary Read and George Featherston, were all real pirates serving with Captain John 'Calico Jack' Rackham, as were the crew-members executed at the end of the book. George Featherston was the Ship's Master and not the bosun but I changed his rank to contrast him with his Royal Navy equivalent in, *Before the Mast.*

The exploits of the pirates are based on true events, other than the involvement of Black Bart Roberts. He was a notorious pirate at the time, but there is no evidence that he had any involvement with Calico Jack. He was known for keeping strict discipline on his ships with no gambling, drinking or women allowed on board. He enforced an early bed-time on his band of cutthroats and forced them to attend church service every Sunday. Naturally most pirates therefore thought him a cruel tyrant. And he did hate the Irish after an Irishman named Kennedy, stole one of his ships.

There really was a *Pirate Code* and *Articles of Agreement,* which set out acceptable behaviour, punishments, and how any plunder would be divided. They usually included compensation for loss of limb or eyes, at a time when injured Royal Navy men would be thrown out to beg (unless they were lucky enough to become a cook). Each of the *Articles* in the book is real, but taken from those of a number of different captains' *Article of Agreements.* It is also true that pirate ships were run as democracies at a time when there was little democracy around in the world. Pirates voted on most decisions and everyone who had signed the *Articles* had an equal vote regardless of age, sex, race, rank or religion. Way ahead of their time. The only time that the crew had to obey the captain was in battle, or in a sea-chase that might lead to battle.

There is some dispute over the name of Calico Jack's ship at the time of his capture. Some sources give it as *Curlew*, but others as *William* or *Neptune.* He sailed in all three at some time or another.

Anne Bonny and Mary Read's strange stories are pretty much as described in the book: Mary decided to start a new life and set sail for America but her ship was attacked by pirates and she joined them, sailing with Calico Jack and Anne Bonny. Rumour had it that she took both of them as lovers.

Along with Anne Bonny, Mary Read did urge Calico Jack to kill Dorothy Thomas when they captured her fishing boat, but he refused. As Mary predicted, this cost them their lives as Dorothy testified against them at their trials. She told the court that Anne Bonny and Mary Read were the most bloodthirsty of Calico Jack's crew and fought and cursed like the rest of them. Mary Read's speech, where she said she approved of hanging pirates as it kept cowards from taking up the profession, was used against her and is recorded in the documents of her trial.

Anne Bonny's father got his maid pregnant with Anne and, instead of abandoning them as a gentleman should, he moved in with them. This caused outrage and his law practice in Cork was boycotted, so they emigrated to America. Anne was a wild girl and put a man in hospital when he tried to take advantage of her when she was just 14. At 16, she eloped with and married James Bonny, a small-time pirate who sold her to Calico Jack when her father cut them off without a penny. James Bonny gave up piracy, took the King's Pardon, and then made a living selling out his old friends who had remained pirates.

When Calico Jack's ship was captured, the men were drunk and cowardly and locked themselves in the fo'c'sle rather than fight. Mary Read was so angry that she fired 2 pistols into the fo'c'sle, killing one and injuring another of the pirates. Only Anne Bonny and Mary Read, along with an unidentified man, (*Scar, in the book*), fought back and tried to repel the boarders, but they were overpowered and taken prisoner. Anne Bonny's last words to Calico Jack before he was hanged were, "*I'm sorry to see you here, but if you had fought like a man you would not now be about to die like a dog. Do straighten yourself up!*"

The crew members caught with Calico Jack were hanged for piracy or mutiny, though not all at the same time and place as in the book. John Eaton and the crew of the pettiagua were also tried and executed for piracy even though there was no real evidence against them.

Anne Bonny and Mary Read avoided hanging by claiming they were pregnant. Their executions were postponed but Mary died in prison of gaol fever. Anne Bonny was never hanged and just disappeared from public records, though there were rumours that her rich father bailed her out and then, under an assumed name, she went back to piracy.

Most hangings around 1720, would not have taken place 'humanely' with a long drop through a trapdoor to break the neck. They would have been hoisted up and left to slowly choke to death. Some condemned prisoners would pay the hangman beforehand to swing on their legs and thereby make their death quicker.

The Governors of The Bahamas and Jamaica, Woodes Rogers and Sir Nicholas Lawes respectively, had a remit to stamp out piracy in the Caribbean, and they did this ruthlessly where any pirates refused the King's Pardon and continued to rob on the high seas. They did this so effectively that 'The Golden Age of Piracy' had come to an end by the close of the decade.

THE IRISH SLAVE TRADE

In the early 1700s, there were as many unfree whites (the majority of them Irish) in the Caribbean as there were African slaves. Many were indentured labourers who sold themselves into servitude for a set number of years in return for passage to the Americas and the promise of land or monetary grant at the end of that period. They could be bought and sold and had no say in where they worked or what they did. However, they did have a light at the end of the tunnel as they knew they would eventually be free, if they lived long enough (many didn't). Years could however be added to their original sentence if they tried to escape or broke rules, so a ruthless owner could extend their servitude at his whim.

Many more, although often classed as such, were **not** indentured labourers as they were transported against their will, sold, beaten and forced to work for no wages or future recompense. This process accelerated during and immediately after Oliver Cromwell's campaign in Ireland (1649-53), and again on a lesser scale after the Glorious Revolution and the Battle of the Boyne in 1690, when thousands of Irish men, women and children were shipped to the West Indies. (This also happened, on a smaller scale, to Scots after the *Battle of Culloden*,

1746).

They included prisoners of war, political prisoners, vagrants, trade unionists, debtors and orphans. Others were simply kidnapped and sold for profit. This was the basis for Robert Louis Stevenson's novel, 'Kidnapped', set in 1751 just after Bonny Prince Charly's rebellion. The hero says, *"...in those days of my youth, white men were still sold into slavery on the plantations and that was the destiny to which my wicked uncle had condemned me."* Although this didn't raise an eyebrow in 1896, when it was published, it is controversial now to call this 'slavery' because some feel it diminishes the enormity of the black slave trade which, in eventual numbers and horror, eclipsed the experience of the Irish and Scots. But if the definition of 'modern slavery' is "the condition of being forced by threats or violence to work for little or no pay and of having no power to control what work you do or where you do it," then what was the Irish experience but slavery? And as late as 1948, in the Universal Declaration of Human Rights, the United Nations banned indentured labour, classing it as a form of slavery.

Fear of the Irish stirring up rebellion, was rife in the Caribbean. After suspecting that Irishmen had been involved in a 1692 slave revolt, Barbadian authorities wrote to the Crown, asking them not to send further *"Irish rebels"* to the colony, *"for we want not labourers of that colour to work for us, but men in whom we may confide, to strengthen us."* This fear led to a policy of divide and rule, with unfree whites no longer working side-by-side with blacks and encouraged to feel superior to them. As they were rebellious, and because they had a nasty habit of dying when working all day under the hot Caribbean sun, the Irish were worth less than Africans. Their owners often valued and treated them accordingly although, unlike African slaves, indentured servants (and even convicts) did have some rights under the law.

There were many people of mixed Irish and African descent in the Caribbean, so I drew Scar from this background to give young Irish lad Dan, a protector.

GLOSSARY

Above board	Pirates often hid most of their crew below the deck (the boards) in order to take a ship by surprise. Ships that displayed their crew openly on deck (above board) were merchantmen not pirates, so it came to mean 'honest'.
Aft	Towards the stern of a ship.
All at sea	Lost.
Articles of Agreement	Code of conduct between the captain and crew of pirate ships, laying out acceptable behaviour, punishments and how any plunder would be divided. They usually included compensation for loss of limb or eyes. (Well ahead of their time).
Bachelor's son	Bastard.
Ballast	Heavy matter placed in a ship's hold to keep it steady when it has no cargo.
Bamboozle	To confuse an enemy by flying false flags.
Bare poles	Ship running without any sails up on the masts.
Barking irons	Pistols.
Beau nasty	Well-dressed but dirty person.
Bedswerver	Adulterer
Binnacle	Box containing the compass of a ship.
Bloody	Swearword. Short for 'By Our Lady'.
Boarders	Sailors who fought their way onto an enemy ship in order to capture it.
Bone box	Mouth.
Bosun (Boatswain)	Warrant Officer who looks after the ship's boats, rigging and flags. Also in charge of everyday discipline on board.
Bow	Pointy end of the ship.
Bow-chaser	Cannon in the bows of ships, pointing forwards. (The only gun that could be fired if you were chasing a ship, hence the name).
Breeches	Pair of trousers cut off at the knee.
Brig	Sailing ship with two masts, both square-rigged.
Broadside	The side of a ship. Usually used to describe all the guns on one side of a warship and their simultaneous discharge.

Bulwark	Defensive railing around the deck of a ship.
Canvas	Sails. These were made from canvas and were sometimes called this.
Carib	Warlike and cannibalistic tribe that once dominated the Caribbean, which was named after them. 'Cannibal' is also derived from 'Carib'.
Cast off	Let go a cable or rope securing a vessel, so that the vessel may make way.
Chainshot	Two solid cannon balls attached to each other by a length of chain. Designed to bring down a ship's masts and rigging.
Chasing wind	Wind coming from directly behind the ship.
Colours	Flags.
Crow's nest	Lookout platform at the masthead. The top of the mainmast.
Cut and run	Cut the anchor chain, for a quick getaway, rather than pulling it slowly on board
Cutlass	Short, broad-bladed, curved sword used at sea.
Dead reckoning	How navigators estimated longitude from approximate speed, tides, currents, winds and direction.
Flogging	Whipping.
Flotsam	Floating wreckage of a ship or its cargo.
Foghorn	Loud horn sounded by ships in fog so other ships wouldn't accidentally ram them.
Frigate	Fast two-deck warship with 30 to 60 cannon, often used for reconnaissance or to carry messages between ships-of-the-line.
Galleon	Large Spanish warship with a high stem and stern.
Gallows	Wooden frame from which is suspended a noose o of rope by which criminals are hanged.
Gallows' jig	The way hanged people kicked their legs as they were slowly strangled, resembled a macabre dance that was called the 'gallows jig' by landsmen, or the 'hempen hornpipe' by sailors, from the hemp rope that was used.
Gangplank	Plank that passengers use to board or exit a ship. Rumour had it that, while at sea, pirates made captives walk the plank to a watery grave.
Gaol	Obsolete spelling of jail.
Gibbet	See 'Gallows'.
Gingamobs	Testicles.

Gunport	Porthole for a gun. These were kept shut for safety except when the guns were to be fired.
Gunwale (Gunnel)	Upper edge of the side of a ship.
Halyard	Rope for hoisting a sail, yard or flag.
Hand	Ordinary crewmember on a ship.
Hawser	Small cable or large rope.
Heads	Ships toilets. Basically, holes in a plank set in the bows and dropping directly into the sea.
Headway	Forward motion of a ship.
Heave to	Bring a ship to a standstill by use of the wind.
Helmsman	Person steering the ship.
Highwater mark	Highest point the tide reaches on a shore, usually marked by a line of seaweed and debris.
Hispaniola	Modern day Haiti and the Dominican Republic.
Hit the deck	Drop suddenly to the ground. Originally a nautical term that moved into general usage.
Holystoning	Cleaning a ship's decks by running heavy stones back and forth across them.
Hull down	Where a ship's hull is hidden over the horizon, and only the sails can be seen.
Isla de los Pinos	Island of the Pines. Present day Isla de los Juvendud.
Jerkin	Close-fitting jacket or waistcoat, usually made of leather.
Jollyboat	Small, ship's boat.
Landlubber	Landsman or inexperienced sailor
Lanthorn	Obsolete spelling of 'lantern'.
Larboard	Left side of a ship. Originally 'load board' – the side of the ship from which you loaded and unloaded cargo, as the steering oar on the 'steer board' side made it difficult to dock on that side. Now called 'port', as larboard and starboard sounded too alike and mistakes could be made.
Latitude	Distance, measured in degrees, North or South of the equator.
League	Distance equal to about 3 nautical miles.
Learn the ropes	People unused to ships had to literally 'learn the ropes' as these controlled the sails, as well as raising/lowering the anchor and securing the ship in port. It came into common usage for learning anything new.
Leeward	Side of the ship opposite to where the wind blows.
Leg irons	Shackles.

Lickspittle	Parasite. An abject flatterer. An arse-kisser.
Linstock	Stick holding the rope-match used to fire a cannon.
Longitude	Distance in degrees, east or west of a standard meridian (usually Greenwich).
Make way	To move ahead.
Man-o-war	A warship.
Maroon	To put ashore on a deserted island or coast and intentionally abandon.
Masthead	The top of the mast.
Matelot	Ordinary seaman below the rank of officer.
Merchantman	Merchant ship.
Mizzenmast	The aft sail on a two-masted vessel.
Muck spout	Foul mouthed person.
Night-soil men	Men who cleaned up the sewage from the streets each night, before towns had sewers.
Pantaloons	Tight trousers.
Pettiagua	Large, flat-bottomed boat, popular with coastal pirates as they could escape into the shallows if pursued. Derived from the Carib word for canoe.
Piece	Musket.
Pike	Old weapon consisting of a long, wooden shaft with a flat, pointed steel tip. (Similar to a spear).
Pitch	Where a ship plunges so that the bow and stern rise and fall alternately.
Plead your belly	Claim you are pregnant. You could escape hanging if you were with child.
Powder monkey	Boy whose job was to keep the ship's cannon supplied with gunpowder.
Press-gang	Body of men used to obtain recruits to the Royal Navy by force.
Pressed man	Someone forced to join a ship against their will.
Unconsecrated	Not blessed by the church.
Rigging	System of ropes and tackle for supporting masts and controlling sails.
Roll	Where a ship sways from side to side.
Rutter	A navigational journal with records of tides, currents, prevailing winds, reefs, islands etc. Sailors used these to help them to navigate.
Roundshot	Solid iron cannonballs.
Sailing close to the wind	Sailing into the wind as near to directly as a sailboat can. This was dangerous in square-riggers because if the wind came round to blow in the front of the sails instead of behind, then they

could be 'taken aback'. i.e. the sails would be pushing in theopposite direction to the ship's momentum and it could shudder to a stop or lose its sails or masts. As it was dangerous it became a saying that someone was, 'sailing close to the wind if they were living dangerously.

Scaffold	See 'Gallows'.
Scurvy	Disease caused by lack of Vitamin C, due to a lack of fresh fruit and vegetables on long voyages. After the 1740s, British ships started to carry lemons or limes to prevent the disease, which is why Americans call the Brits 'Limeys'.
Sheet	Rope attached to the lower lee corner of a sail to extend it into the wind. It can also refer to the sail.
Ship's biscuit	Biscuits that were double-baked to make them last longer for voyages. The problem was that it made them so hard they were difficult to bite into.
Ship's log	Official diary kept by the captain.
Shore battery	Anti-ship artillery in coastal fortification.
Skeleton crew	Minimum crew needed to sail a ship.
Spinnaker	Large sail deployed at the front of a boat when there's a chasing wind.
Spoils	Spoils of war. In the case of pirate ships, plunder.
Starboard	Right side of a ship. In days of old, the steering oar was on the right side which became known as the 'steer board' or 'starboard' side.
Stern	Backside of a ship.
Stern-chaser	As with 'bow-chaser' but sited in the stern to fire at pursuing (chasing) vessels.
Strike the colours	Pull down the flag and surrender a ship.
Square-rigged	Fitted with square-shaped sails. They work well with a chasing wind but are not good at sailing close to the wind where triangular sails, as on modern yachts, are better.
Tack	Sailing ships could not sail directly into the wind or they would be Taken Aback. To make way in the direction of the wind they had to zigzag into the general direction of the wind.
Taken aback	Where sailing ships were sailing close to the wind, if the wind came round to blow in the front of the sails instead of behind, then they could be 'taken aback'. i.e. the sails would be pushing in the opposite direction to the ship's momentum and it

	could shudder to a stop or lose its sails or masts. This led to the saying, 'taken aback' when the idea was applied to people metaphorically.
Topmen	The most agile and experienced sailors who would climb highest in the rigging to furl and unfurl the topsails. They were higher paid than the waisters who stayed on deck in the waist of the ship.
Toss pot	Drunkard. Someone who tosses back pots of ale.
Touch-hole	Hole at the top rear of a cannon through which the gunpowder was ignited.
Tow rag	Cloth for wiping your bum. It was tied to the end of a rope and dragged along in the sea to keep it clean between uses, hence the name. If someone calls you a 'tow rag', now you know what it means.
Weather gage	Upwind of another vessel. It is the advantageous position for a fighting sailing ship to be in as the ship with the weather gage can manoeuvre at will, whereas the other vessel would have to tack if it wanted to close on the other ship.
Went about	Turned into the wind onto an opposite tack.
Yard	Long beam on a ship for spreading sails on.
Yardarm	The end of the yard.

If you enjoyed this book then please take a minute to
leave an honest review at:

AMAZON.CO.UK
HOIST THE BLACK FLAG: The Adventures of Dan Leake
J.R. MULHOLLAND

www.amazon.co.uk/dp/B08X6DXQ9T

Keep your eye out for the other two books in the trilogy,
Before the Mast and *The Pirate Republic*.

Thanks for reading.

J.R. Mulholland

www.jrmulholland.co.uk

Printed in Great Britain
by Amazon